He'd been shocked to see Jen in the church

After leaving town more than ten years ago, Walker had never expected to see her again. Never wanted to.

Memories slammed into him like an unexpected fist. Apparently he hadn't forgotten about Jen after all.

Did she even remember what she'd done to him?

As if she sensed his approach, Jen looked up and stilled. She stared at him, and he saw a jumble of emotions cross her face—shock, distress, dread.

And shame.

So...she hadn't forgotten.

Dear Reader,

We all have one thing in the past that haunts us. The thing we want to go back and change, the mistake that seems to be irreversible. There's a wrong we committed, an error we made, a person we hurt. No one makes it through life without regrets.

We can't rewrite history, but a few of us are lucky enough to have a chance to confront our failings again. Older and wiser, the second time around we can face the person we harmed and atone for our sins.

Jen Summers has always regretted what she did to Walker Barnes in high school. When he returns to Otter Tail for Quinn Murphy and Maddie Johnson's wedding, she's forced to deal with him again. Life takes a very unexpected turn for these two people, and I loved watching them maneuver through rough water.

I hope you enjoy my second visit to Otter Tail, Wisconsin. Please let me know what you think of Jen and Walker's story at my Web site, www.margaretwatson.com, or e-mail me at margaret@margaretwatson.com. I love hearing from readers!

Margaret Watson

Can't Stand the Heat?
Margaret Watson

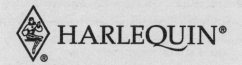

TORONTO • NEW YORK • LONDON
AMSTERDAM • PARIS • SYDNEY • HAMBURG
STOCKHOLM • ATHENS • TOKYO • MILAN • MADRID
PRAGUE • WARSAW • BUDAPEST • AUCKLAND

Recycling programs
for this product may
not exist in your area.

ISBN-13: 978-0-373-71638-8

CAN'T STAND THE HEAT?

Copyright © 2010 by Margaret Watson.

Printed in U.S.A.

ABOUT THE AUTHOR

Margaret Watson has always made up stories in her head. When she started actually writing them down, she realized she'd found exactly what she wanted to do with the rest of her life. Almost twenty years after staring at that first blank page, she's an award-winning, two-time RITA® Award finalist who has written more than twenty books for Silhouette and Harlequin.

When she's not writing or spending time with her family, she practices veterinary medicine. She loves everything about her job, other than the "Hey, Dr. Watson, where's Sherlock?" jokes, which she's heard way too many times. She loves pets, but writing is her passion. And that's just elementary, my dear readers.

Margaret spends as much time as possible visiting the area that inspires her books, the Door County, Wisconsin, cities of Algoma and Sturgeon Bay. When she's not eating Door County cherries, smoked fish and cheese, she lives in a Chicago suburb with her husband, three daughters and a menagerie of pets.

Books by Margaret Watson

HARLEQUIN SUPERROMANCE

*The McKinnes Triplets

For my story conference partners,
Lindsay Longford and Julie Wachowski.
You're the best. And you know why.

CHAPTER ONE

"WHO'S THE EXTRA GUY?" Jen nudged Maddie as she peered out from behind her friend in the tiny private room off the church vestibule. Her friend looked up from adjusting her blue garter as Jen studied the back of the tall, broad-shouldered man in the gray suit. His dark blond hair brushed the collar of his shirt, and his crisply tailored pants broke sharply over a pair of neon-green-and-orange running shoes.

Whoever he was, he sure didn't live in Otter Tail.

The calm, beautiful notes of Bach's "Air on a G String" floated out of the church's sanctuary as Maddie dropped the folds of her wedding gown and straightened. "Walker," she cried, dashing out the door to embrace him. "You made it!"

The man turned around and swept Maddie off her feet. "You think I'd miss Quinn's wedding? Not a chance."

Jen's bouquet slipped out of her hands and

landed on the marble floor. A red rose petal bounced onto the toe of her shoe.

Walker?

That couldn't possibly be Walker Barnes.

Could it?

In high school, Walker's face had been soft. Unfinished. The features of a kid who spent most of his time in front of a computer.

Now his face was lean and hard, as if a sculptor had carved away the excess to reveal the angles and planes.

The rest of his body matched his face.

He was talking to Maddie and smiling, and his green eyes sparkled. Jen couldn't tear her gaze away from him. He looked happy. Relaxed.

He looked like Walker Barnes all grown up. Transformed into a handsome man with a toughness the younger Walker hadn't had.

A Walker she didn't recognize.

"Jen? You all right?" The other bridesmaid touched her arm.

Jen adjusted the skirt of her black silk dress as she bent to retrieve her bouquet. "I'm fine, Delaney. Nervous, I guess." She smoothed one bent rose petal and pinched off a broken piece of baby's breath. "I think I need a drink." Delaney raised her eyebrows. "Of water," Jen added hastily.

Maddie kissed Walker's cheek and whispered something in his ear. He nodded as he disappeared out the front door of the church. Then Maddie turned to Jen and Delaney. "Are you guys ready?"

"Whenever you are," Delaney answered.

Maddie glanced into the church and stilled. She was looking at Quinn, standing at the altar, waiting for her. "I'm ready. I've been ready for months," she said softly.

Had Jen ever felt that way? As if she'd die if she couldn't have Tony?

She had, but getting married had killed that passion. Yet she'd survived.

Delaney stepped through the doorway, the pianist began playing "Jesu, Joy of Man's Desiring," and Delaney started down the aisle.

"Anything you need?" Jen whispered to Maddie, trying to focus on her friend instead of the man who had mysteriously appeared in the church. "Any last-minute fixes?"

"I need only one thing," Maddie answered. As she moved to the door at the back of the church, she was focused only on Quinn, and her joy was blinding.

Jen swallowed the sudden lump in her throat and turned to begin her own walk down the aisle.

There was a second man standing next to Quinn now. Walker? He was in the wedding?

"Maddie. What's Walker Barnes doing up there?"

"He and Quinn are friends," Maddie whispered. "We weren't sure he'd make it in time." She nudged Jen. "Pretty hot, isn't he? I'll make sure we get some pictures of the two of you together so you can get reacquainted."

Reacquainted? Oh, my God. Maddie's perfect wedding was turning into Jen's worst nightmare.

Delaney had nearly reached the front of the church by the time Jen took her first step into the aisle. Instead of watching where she was going, she was staring at Walker, so she didn't miss his shock when he recognized her. She tripped on a tiny ripple in the thin carpet that had been unrolled down the aisle.

A desperate grab at the edge of a pew saved her from falling on her face. Taking a deep breath, she stared straight ahead at the minister.

It's not about you.

Not about Walker.

Don't spoil this for Quinn and Maddie.

She reached the front of the church and stood next to Delaney, then turned to watch the bride. The pianist shifted to "Ode To Joy," Maddie stepped through the door and everyone rose.

Maddie was luminous. Radiant. There was no

hesitation in her walk, no doubt in her expression. A tiny part of Jen was envious that Maddie had found her dream. Jen's had shattered years ago.

The minister's words washed over her as she listened to the traditional ceremony, the vows, the promises. Jen's eyes blurred again, and she squeezed them shut. She didn't cry at weddings anymore.

The church erupted in cheers, and Jen jerked her attention back to the present. Maddie and Quinn were kissing, then held hands as they walked down the aisle. Delaney stuck her arm through Paul's, the other groomsman, and they followed the bride and groom.

Jen drew in a deep breath, then looked across at Walker. His face was expressionless, impossible to read. He stepped forward and held out his arm, and she reached to take it.

Her fingers hovered in the air as she looked into his green eyes. Nothing. She had no idea what he was thinking.

He put his other hand over hers. His fingers were warm and callused, and his arm beneath the wool suit was solid as a rock.

"Snap out of it," he said in a harsh whisper. "Let's go."

She ignored the thundering of her heart beneath

the black cocktail dress. Surely he could hear it. The whole church must be able to hear it.

The scent of the outdoors drifted off him and mingled with the perfume of her bouquet. She didn't remember how he'd smelled before. She wasn't sure she'd ever noticed.

She'd been the same height as Walker in high school. Now he towered over her as they moved down the aisle. He walked easily, as if having Jen's hand on his arm was no big deal. Her own shoulders were tense, her muscles tight. Thank God she had an excuse to leave as soon as they reached the back of the church.

As soon as they stepped through the doors at the rear of the sanctuary, she snatched her hand away. She ducked around him, but Walker grasped her arm.

"Running away, Jen? You're going to miss all the fun."

She stepped out of his reach, grabbed her purse from the small office where they'd waited and left the church.

Her hands shook as she tried to start her car. She managed to shove the key into the slot, but then turned it too hard. The starter groaned, the engine revved and the car bucked as she engaged the clutch and pulled out of the parking lot.

What was going on? How had Walker Barnes ended up at Maddie and Quinn's wedding? Jen hadn't thought about him in years. No one ever talked about him. He'd left town ages ago, and as far as she knew, he'd never been back.

She chewed on the inside of her cheek as she drove the few blocks to the reception site. She could handle this. He'd be at the reception, but she could avoid him. She'd stay in the kitchen until Maddie needed her for pictures.

He'd want to avoid her, too. Remembered shame made her cringe. Neither one of them would want to revisit what had happened in high school. She wasn't the same person now. And neither was Walker.

At least not physically.

And somewhere in the past fourteen years, he'd become self-assured. He'd added self-confidence to his formidable intelligence.

In any other man, it would be a killer combo.

She shuddered as she stopped beside city hall, parking next to the van she'd borrowed to deliver the food. The reception was in the ballroom on the top floor of the converted mansion. It was where most of the town's wedding receptions were held.

She was supplying the food, and she had to forget about Walker and concentrate on her job. This was vital, she reminded herself. It was the first step in her plan.

Her eldest son, Nick, was already here, setting up. She slammed the car door and hurried into the building.

Her first catering job *would* go smoothly. She'd spent hours planning the smallest details.

Nick would have the chafing dishes heating, as she'd instructed. She'd take care of the finishing touches and everything would be ready when the crowd arrived.

Her stomach untwisted. It was going to be okay. She would be too busy to think about Walker. And if she was very lucky, by the time she finished in the kitchen he would have left town again.

As she hurried into the ballroom, she saw the line of chafing dishes on the white-clothed tables, just like they were supposed to be, and she relaxed some more. Okay. Good.

But she couldn't smell any appetizing aromas. If the food was warm, she should smell it. Walking faster, she reached the tables and found that the chafing dishes hadn't been lit. The pans of food were in place, but they were cold.

"Nick! Where are you?"

"In here," he called from the small kitchen in the far corner.

"You didn't light the Sterno. Nothing's ready."

"I couldn't find anything to light them with." He strolled out of the kitchen, holding his video game.

She pushed past him into the room and yanked open a drawer. "You didn't see these?" She held up a box of matches.

"I was looking for one of those lighter things."

She flicked on the burners of the ancient stove. "Go get those pans."

He pushed a button twice on his video game as he stared at the screen. "Jeez. No one's even here yet."

"Did I interrupt you? I'm sorry." She clamped her mouth shut and closed her eyes, reaching for patience. Sarcasm was lost on a teenager. "Start hauling the food in here, or that game unit is history."

He rolled his eyes, but set the game on a counter and went and got a pan.

"Nick, I am *paying* you to do this. Do you understand the concept of working to earn money?"

He plopped the pan on the stove. "God, Mom. Chill."

Fifteen minutes later, the food was heated through and replaced in the now-lit chafing dishes. Jen was plating the spring rolls when she heard voices in the outer room.

"Nick, are the plates and silverware out?"

He didn't look up from his spot against the counter as he played his game. "Duh, Mom. You told me to do it ten minutes ago."

She took a deep breath. She had to calm down. "Sorry. But you need to put that away. We're going to be busy."

"As soon as I finish this level." His fingers flew over the tiny buttons.

"That's it. Give it to me."

She held out her hand, waiting, and he scowled as he slapped it into her palm. "What do you want me to do?"

"Make sure the Sterno is still lit. Put out the serving spoons." She shoved the game into her tote bag. "Set up the sauces in front of each pan. Then go stand out there, in case anyone wants to know what the dishes are. Do you remember what everything is?"

"You told me ten times already."

"Just making sure." Not only was it her first catering job, but it was her friends' wedding. Everything had to be perfect.

The next forty-five minutes passed in a blur of cooking and serving interrupted by posing for pictures. As she watched Sarah, the woman she'd hired to help with the event, carry the last pan of artichoke-and-cheese-stuffed mushrooms to the table, Tony, her ex-husband, walked over.

"Great food, Jen. When did you learn to cook like this?"

She'd always been able to cook like this. But Tony had rarely been home to eat with them. "Here and there," she said lightly.

"I can't believe Walker Barnes was in the wedding. Who ever thought he'd show up in town again?"

"I noticed. Did you talk to him?"

"Barnes? Hell, no. That wasn't the proudest moment of my life."

Hers, either. Time to change the subject. "Nick's working really hard," she whispered.

"Good for him."

"Maybe you could say something to him. Pretend like you'd noticed?" she said a little too sharply.

"Okay." Tony sounded surprised, as if the concept of complimenting his older son for doing a good job had never occurred to him. It probably hadn't—catering wasn't a sport.

Why was she getting worked up? She and Tony had already had this fight. Way too often.

Time to move on. "What's Tommy doing?"

"He's running around with a couple of his buddies."

Translation: Tony had no idea what his younger

son was doing. "Round him up and send him over, would you? I haven't seen him since everyone got here."

"Sure, Jen." Munching on a spear of tenderloin-wrapped asparagus, Tony ambled off.

"Tommy's okay, Mom," Nick said in a low voice. "He's playing tag in the hall."

"Thanks, Nick." She smiled at him. Just when she was completely exasperated with her teenage son, he did something thoughtful and mature, like watch out for his brother. "I appreciate that you checked."

Nick scowled. "I didn't *check* on him. I saw him there through the door."

"I still appreciate it." She turned off the burner underneath the last pan of roasted-corn quesadillas. "Take this out to the table, will you?"

"Okay."

She followed him to the ballroom and bent to pick up a serving spoon that had fallen to the floor.

"Sweet shoes, man," she heard her son say.

Crouched on the floor, hidden by the table skirt, Jen saw a pair of green-and-orange running shoes.

CHAPTER TWO

"THANKS." Walker glanced down at the running shoes. He'd been a little embarrassed to wear them, but not enough to buy another pair. "Forgot to bring my dress shoes."

"I would have worn them on purpose."

Walker took another look at the kid. His shaggy blond hair framed a face that was a mix of child and adult. He was all arms and legs, and his green eyes caught Walker's attention. The kid looked familiar. As if Walker had seen him before. Which was impossible, since he hadn't been back here in more than ten years.

He must be the son of someone Walker had known back then.

Paul, the other groomsman, the guy with the thousand-dollar suit and the ponytail, walked up to the buffet, saving Walker from the odd impulse to ask the kid his name. "What's good, Nick?" he asked.

"Everything, Mr. Black. My mom's an awesome cook."

Nice. Not many teens would compliment their mother in public. Walker tasted a stuffed mushroom as he wandered off, and raised his eyebrows. The boy was right. She was a great cook.

Walker glanced at his watch. Close to 5:00 p.m. If he left now, he could make it back to Chicago tonight.

He could stop by the cemetery to finally visit his father's grave at long last, on his way out of town.

As he headed for the door of the ballroom, Quinn hurried over. "You're not leaving, are you?"

"Yeah. Sorry. I have to get back for a meeting tomorrow."

"On a Sunday?" The groom raised his eyebrows, and Walker shrugged.

"Busted. There's no meeting. But I'm guessing you and Maddie are going to be busy for a while."

Quinn glanced over to where his bride was talking to a group of friends. "Yeah, we'll be busy," he said softly. "But we're not going anywhere. We just reopened the pub and we have to work."

"You're going back to work? Tomorrow? Instead of taking a honeymoon?"

"A honeymoon is a state of mind, Barnes," he said, still watching his wife.

Walker would have said the poor fool was whipped. But Maddie got the same expression on her face when she looked at her new husband.

"I'm happy for you guys. Really I am. But I'm going to go."

"You can't. There's more wedding stuff Maddie wants to do."

"Like what? You said 'I do,' we toasted you, pictures were taken, we ate. What else is there?"

"You need to rein in those romantic tendencies of yours, Barnes." Quinn clapped him on the back. "We have more pictures to take."

As Walker reluctantly followed his friend, he spotted Jen in the group around Maddie. *Romantic.*

No, he wasn't that.

He'd been shocked to see Jen in the church. He'd never expected to see her again. Never wanted to. Now, he couldn't help noticing that her blond hair wasn't as bright as it used to be, or as long. It was still curly, though, and she still wore it in a ponytail. She looked tired, but she was even curvier than she'd been in high school. And just as beautiful. People milled around her, but Jen was the only one he noticed.

All the feelings he'd forgotten for so long came surging back—his stupid infatuation with her, how gullible he'd been when she'd pleaded for a favor.

The sex she'd used to pay him for it.

The despair he'd felt when his escape from Otter Tail had been cut off.

Apparently he hadn't forgotten about Jen, after all.

Did she even remember what she'd done to him? And where was Tony? They'd been inseparable in high school. Except for that one memorable episode in the janitor's closet.

As if she sensed his approach, Jen looked up and stilled. Her gaze locked on his, and he saw a jumble of emotions cross her face.

So she hadn't forgotten.

"I need some pictures." Maddie herded them toward the flowers massed at the end of the table holding the cake. "Then I'll cut the cake and we can finally dance."

He could finally leave.

He followed the photographer's directions dutifully, standing with her and Quinn, with the other attendants, with Quinn by himself. Then Maddie said, "Paul? Delaney? How about one of you two?"

The man in the expensive suit draped his arm over the short blonde's shoulders, and they grinned at the camera. Walker looked at Jen and found her gazing at him. She quickly glanced away.

He hoped Maddie didn't expect him to get chummy with Jen. That wasn't going to happen.

Although she was a knockout in the black, low-cut dress. She'd pulled her hair out of the ponytail and it fell in waves to her shoulders. He'd always had a soft spot for blondes in black dresses. He had very fond memories of Barb in a low-cut black dress at the gala they'd attended last week.

She drew in a deep, shaky breath that emphasized her cleavage. He reminded himself that he wasn't interested in how well she filled out the dress.

"It's been a long time, Jen," he said.

"It has. How are you?"

"I'm good." He would be even better when he was back home in Chicago. "How's Tony?" he asked.

She slid her right hand over her left. "He's here, so you can ask him yourself."

He grabbed a cup of punch from the cake table and handed it to her. When she reached for it, he saw she wasn't wearing a ring.

"Are you guys divorced?"

She dropped her hand. "Yes."

"Sorry to hear that." He set the cup back on the table.

"Are you?" Her voice was so quiet he could barely hear her above the crowd noise. Had she even meant to speak out loud?

"Any kids?" Walker tried not to grimace as he spoke. This was his definition of hell—making polite conversation with Jen.

"Two sons." Her expression softened. "That's Tommy," she said, pointing to a dark-haired boy dodging among the guests, chasing another kid.

He was the image of Tony, who was trying to corral him. "Cute."

"Thank you."

Maddie was laughing at something the other attendants were saying. *Let's move this along so I can get out of here.*

Tony walked up to Jen just then, his face red, his jaw clenched. "He's out of control."

"That's because you let him have three cupcakes," she retorted. She bit her lip and said, "Tony, you remember Walker Barnes."

Tony stared at Walker. "Hey. How's it going?"

"Just great," he said. "How about you?"

"I'm good."

The uncomfortable silence stretched too long. Might as well make it worse. "How did the baseball thing work out for you?"

Tony clenched his hands into fists. "I played in the minors for a few years until I blew out my shoulder. I was on track to be called up when it happened."

"That's too bad," Walker said. "What are you doing now?"

"I'm a cop." He looked Walker up and down, his gaze lingering on his shoes. "How about you?"

"I write video games."

"Yeah?" His expression said it was too bad the job didn't pay him enough to afford a pair of dress shoes.

Walker smiled. "You a cop here in Otter Tail?"

"Green Bay."

"Walker, Jen, it's your turn," Maddie called.

He nodded at Tony and walked to the spot the other couple had vacated. Jen moved next to him, standing stiff and straight, staying as far away as she could.

"Can you two at least act as if you like each other?" the photographer called.

They both shifted an inch. "A little more," she said, peering through the viewfinder.

Jen's arm brushed the sleeve of his coat, and she twitched away, as if she couldn't bear touching him. That did it. He wrapped his arm around her shoulder and tugged her against him.

"How about this?" he asked the photographer.

"Perfect." She beamed.

Jen strained away from him, but he held on to her and kept smiling. She was pinned to his side, her shoulder digging into his ribs. When she shifted her leg so their thighs weren't touching, he tightened his grip. Her skin was silky smooth and the muscles tensing beneath his fingers were surprisingly strong.

"You didn't introduce me to your other son," he said softly, still smiling at the camera. He hadn't seen another Tony clone running around.

"I'm not sure where he is."

"He didn't come to the wedding?"

She tried to move away again. "He was helping me serve the food. When we were done, he disappeared into some corner with his friends. Teenage boys don't hang around their parents."

"You made the food?"

"I did."

"It was really good." He squeezed her arm, and smiled when she flinched and tried to pull away.

His smile faded as her hair fluttered around her shoulders. It still smelled like lemons. He'd dreamed of lemons after that interlude in the closet. "You're a woman of hidden talents, aren't you?"

"Let go of me right now or I'm going to hurt you," she said through clenched teeth as she continued to smile.

"Maddie wants pictures. We need to make nice for the camera."

"Maddie's gotten all the pictures she's going to

get." Jen jerked free, and this time he let her go. Her momentum made her stumble, but she caught herself quickly.

He watched her retreat, his gaze lingering on the sway of her hips in her snug dress. Who knew it would be so much fun to torment Jen Summers?

An older couple stopped her and said something, and her shoulders relaxed. Then another woman came by and smiled. Jen had a lot of friends in town. She was still the popular girl.

And he was still the outsider. But this time he was more than happy to keep it that way.

"It wouldn't kill you to stick around for a couple more days," Quinn said quietly at his elbow. "You haven't even seen our pub."

"I'm sure it's a great pub. But there are too many memories in this town for me, and none of them are good," he replied.

"So make some new ones. It's not a bad place, Walker."

"What's the point?"

"Friendship, maybe?" Quinn said. "We can't get to Chicago for a while. And I know damn well you're not coming back here."

"Not until your first kid is baptized," he answered. "So you and Maddie better get busy if you want to see me again."

"Suit yourself. Just say goodbye before you leave."

Quinn headed toward Maddie, as if they were attached by a giant rubber band. If they got too far apart, it pulled them back together.

Was Barb tugging him back to Chicago? Of course she was. Especially if she wore that black dress again the next time they went out.

Walker's footsteps slowed as he went to the door. The sky was darkening outside the ballroom windows, and in a few minutes it would be too late to visit the cemetery. It wouldn't kill him to stay the night.

He'd slept in worse places than the Bide-a-Wee Motel. The business he needed to attend to could wait another day. If he stayed, his conscience would stop nagging him about visiting his father's grave.

And Barb would still be there tomorrow.

As he stood in the doorway, he spotted the kid from the buffet table with two boys about his age, and once again was struck by the sense of familiarity. As if he *knew* him. Then he remembered what Jen had said—that her other son had helped her serve the food.

This was Jen's son? He looked nothing like his brother. Or Tony. He had Jen's blond hair, but that was the only resemblance Walker saw.

As he watched, Jen's son elbowed one of the

other boys and grinned. Walker sucked in a breath. It was like looking at a picture of his father as a teen.

How old *was* Jen's son?

"You're still here." Quinn's voice.

Walker continued to stare at the boy. "I've changed my mind. I'm going to stick around for a while."

CHAPTER THREE

WALKER WAS STALKING HER.

Sitting at her own kitchen table, she could think of nothing else. It had been two days since the wedding, and he'd been at the Harp both nights.

Asking about her.

Jen knew, because Maddie had come into the pub kitchen at least three times, reminding her to join them after she closed up.

Yeah, as if that was going to happen.

She'd left through the back door and gotten Jorge, the dishwasher, to lock it behind her.

Did sneaking away make her a coward?

Hell, no. It made her smart. Strong. In charge of herself.

All she wanted to do was forget about Walker Barnes. Again. Put him out of her mind and get on with her life. Eventually, she wouldn't even remember he'd been at the wedding.

It couldn't happen soon enough. He'd already cost her two nights' sleep.

He wouldn't cost her a third. He had to be gone. It was Tuesday afternoon, so he'd already missed at least one day of work.

He'd probably left Otter Tail after the pub closed last night and headed back to wherever he lived. She hadn't asked. She hadn't wanted to know.

"Tommy! Nick! Where are you?" she yelled. Her mother, who was standing at the sink, raised her eyebrows, and Jen shrugged.

She jerked the laces of her softball shoes a little tighter. Why weren't either of her sons ready to go? She was the coach. She couldn't be late to baseball practice.

"I have to do homework," Nick answered.

"This isn't negotiable. You know that." Jen poked her head into the dining room, where her older son was lounging against the computer desk, playing his handheld video game.

He scowled as he straightened. "This is totally lame."

"Lame or not, you're going to run while I'm at Tommy's baseball practice. That's the deal. It's been the deal since the season started. So put your running shoes on."

He stared at her for a long moment, then grabbed

his shoes and walked, barefoot, out to the car. As she watched him, her younger son dashed into the room, holding his bat and mitt. "Ready, Mom."

"Where's your water bottle, honey?"

"Oops." Tommy dropped his equipment and rummaged in a cabinet.

"I'll get it, Tommy," Jen's mom said. "You get your things together for practice."

"Thanks, Mom," Jen said as she stood up. "And thanks for starting dinner."

"You're a much better cook than I am, Jen. But I still know how to put a meal on the table."

Jen kissed her mom's cheek, then yanked open the door and headed for the car.

Her head was pounding. Running around outside with a bunch of eleven-year-olds was exactly what she needed.

Nick was already in the back when she got into the car, and she sighed. She never would have imagined missing the days when Nick and Tommy fought over who got to ride in front. Now, at fifteen years old, Nick preferred the backseat, where he could play his video games, listen to his music and pretend he couldn't hear her.

Tommy ran out of the house, his water bottle clutched in one hand and his gear in the other. "Shotgun!" he shouted as he scrambled into the car.

"Big whoop-di-doo," Nick said. "Shotgun is for losers."

Tommy knelt on the seat to face his brother. "You're just mad because Mom is making you come to my practice and run."

"Shut up, butthead." Nick jammed earbuds into his ears and turned on his mp3 player.

"Stop it, both of you." Jen closed her eyes for a moment. "Tommy, turn around and put on your seat belt. Nick, don't talk to your brother like that." She threw the car into gear and backed out of the drive-way.

By the time they reached the park, she'd managed to calm herself, lost in her thoughts. Catering the wedding had been the first step. She'd needed to see how she handled cooking for a lot of people all at once.

She'd handled it just fine. Several people at the wedding had told her they were going to try her menu at the Harp. One of Maddie's friends from Sturgeon Falls had tentatively hired her to cater a party.

Which was great, but Jen didn't want a career as a caterer. She wanted to open her own restaurant. She just needed more money first.

Tommy jumped out of the car and ran to the handful of boys already standing on the baseball diamond. Nick pretended he didn't know they'd arrived.

"Nick."

When she turned around, he reluctantly put the game on the car seat. "Get it over with," she said gently. "Pretend it was your idea. All of Tommy's friends think you're cool." She smiled at him. "Next time, I bet some of them will run with you."

He snorted, but pulled his shoes on and got out, then began jogging the perimeter of the field.

As she watched him run, his white headphone wires bouncing, his stiff, resentful posture gradually relaxed. Nick had refused to get involved in any organized sports this year. All he wanted to do was play video games and sit at the computer. Tony had pitched a fit, but Jen knew Nick had always hated organized sports. He'd only played soccer and baseball to get his father's approval.

So she'd made him a deal. He could drop the sports, but he needed exercise. He would come to every baseball practice and game with her and Tommy, and he'd run. When he'd gone three miles, he could play his video games and have access to the computer.

No one ever told you that parenting was a series of compromises. That it required the negotiation skills of a lawyer and the patience of a saint.

She was becoming an expert at the negotiation part.

Slamming the door shut, she hoisted the bag of

bats and balls over her shoulder. The boys were chasing one another around home plate. "Okay, guys, let's get started."

ANOTHER PRACTICE FINISHED without a disaster or a meltdown.

Miraculous, when you were dealing with eleven-year-olds.

Nick was already in the car, slouching against the door. Jen called to Tommy, "Come on, bud. Grandma's fixing dinner and I want to help her." Afterward, she was going to work on a new recipe for duck, and if it worked, she'd add it to her "dishes for the restaurant" file.

Her younger son waved, but kept talking to one of his friends as he walked toward her. Making dinner was supposed to be her contribution to living with her parents. She needed to finish up for her mom.

Finally Tommy reached them. He threw his bag on the floor of the backseat, then climbed into the front. "You promised we could go to Frank's after practice."

Damn it. She'd forgotten about that. "Could we do it tomorrow, honey?"

"It won't take long. I already know what I want."

She glanced over at her sports-mad son. "Whose card are you buying this time?"

"A-Rod's," he told her. "The best player in baseball."

"Do you have enough money for that?"

"Grandma paid me to dig up the garden. I've been saving up for it."

"Okay," Jen sighed. "But it has to be quick."

"It will be," he said happily. He turned in his seat to face his brother. "Too bad they don't have computer-game cards."

Without looking up, Nick said, "Dork."

Jen pulled to the curb in front of the sports memorabilia shop. "Let's go, Tommy."

As he ran into the store, she noticed a going-out-of-business sign in the window. Her interest piqued, she stepped back and looked the place over. This would be a perfect spot for a restaurant. On the main street, right in the middle of downtown.

The bell over the door chimed as she walked in. Tommy was deep in discussion with Frank Jones, and she looked around the shop. The high ceiling was covered with pressed tin, and the walls had a painted wooden wainscoting. The hardwood floor was scratched, but the wood was beautiful.

Too bad Frank couldn't wait another few months to close. This space was exactly what she wanted.

A blast of cool air rushed in as the door chimed

behind her. "Give me a break," she said as she turned, "he's almost…"

It wasn't Nick. "Walker. What are you doing here?"

"I was walking by and saw you. Thought I'd say hello." He smiled, but it didn't extend to his eyes.

Walker Barnes was the last thing she needed tonight. "Let's go, Tommy."

She maneuvered past Walker and held open the door for her son. She got in the car, waited for Tommy to fasten his seat belt and drove away.

SHE COULDN'T RUN OUT the door at her own home.

Walker's Porsche rolled to a stop in front of a small, tidy house on a quiet street. Quinn had told him Jen was living with her parents. The white two-story with black shutters and an enclosed front porch looked as if it hadn't changed at all.

Back in high school, he'd driven past her house too many times to count, hoping to catch a glimpse of her. He'd been a stupid kid with a crush on the popular, gorgeous Jen.

What an idiot he'd been.

After high school, he'd thought all Jen Summers had stolen was his ticket out of Otter Tail. After seeing her kid at the wedding, he wondered if she'd stolen something far more precious.

His son.

The slam of his car door echoed in his ears as he climbed the steps to the glassed-in porch and opened the storm door. The macramé plant holder hanging above a wicker love seat held a blue pot with a few dead stems sticking straight up. The floral cushion on the loveseat was faded from the sun, and someone had put a piece of duct tape over a tear in the fabric. A child's bike lay propped against the wall on the opposite side of the porch, behind two wicker chairs. They looked newer, but a thin film of dust covered all the furniture.

She neglected her parents' house. So did her parents... How well did they take care of her kids?

He punched the doorbell and waited. A small beater of a car, an ugly brown thing mottled with rust spots, sat in the driveway. The same one she'd driven away from the church in on Saturday. She must be home. He hit the doorbell again.

Finally he heard the sound of footsteps. Moments later, the door opened. Jen's older son stood there.

His son?

Walker searched the boy's face, looking for a clue. Was *his* nose that shape? Were *his* cheekbones that high, that sharp? How did you look at another person and see yourself in his face? If this was his child, shouldn't he be feeling something? A sense of connection? Of attachment?

All he felt was unnerved. Angry.

Behind thick glasses, the kid's eyes were green, but not the same green as Walker's. They narrowed. Did this boy see it, too? The resemblance?

"Yeah?" he asked.

"Is Jen here?"

The kid frowned. "I saw you at the wedding. You had the cool shoes."

"I'm Walker Barnes. Is she home?"

The kid stared at him. "Walker Barnes? No way." He took a step closer. "Are you shitting me?"

"Why would I do that?" Walker asked cautiously.

"I mean, are you, like, *the* Walker Barnes? The dude who owns GeekBoy? The guy who wrote *Blade* and *Demonfire* and *Armageddon*? Why would Walker Barnes want to see my mom?"

"Yeah, that's me." Gripping the doorjamb, Walker searched Nick's face again.

He should feel it now. The bond. But he didn't.

The teen's eyes had gone huge behind his thick glasses. "Awesome. Man, Davy is going to be sooo bummed he left. Wait until I tell him who he missed."

Stupid to think he'd feel some mystical link. Or that Nick would. All Nick saw was the guy who'd written his favorite games.

"Could you tell your mom I'm here first?"

"Right. Yeah. Okay. Just a minute." He started away from the door, then turned back. "Oh, come in. You don't have to wait on the porch."

Nick took off, yelling, "Mom! Mom! Come here!"

CHAPTER FOUR

WALKER GLANCED AROUND the living room. A green recliner stood against one wall, and it looked as if it had been there for a while. There was a worn spot on the footrest and a dark stain on the arm of the chair.

The light blue denim couch was newer. A compact disc player trailed headphones onto the floor. He hadn't seen one of those gadgets in years— everyone he knew had the latest iPod. A computer sat on a small, paper-covered desk between the living room and dining room.

A bat, several baseballs and a catcher's mitt lay jumbled on the worn carpet.

The place was messy. Lived in. Comfortable.

Worlds away from his tidy, professionally decorated condo. No clutter dared challenge his housekeeper.

Photos stood on a bookcase at the end of the room, and Walker picked up one frame that held at least ten pictures of Nick. School pictures, probably. Had Walker's mother kept his in a frame, so prominently displayed?

He didn't remember.

In the first shot, Nick was a child with light blond hair and chubby cheeks, wearing a dress shirt and grinning at the camera.

Eyeglasses had been added three pictures later. By the seventh one, the boy's hair had gotten darker, and the dress shirt and grin had disappeared. In the last photo, he wore a baggy T-shirt and scowled at the camera.

Ten pictures. All Walker knew about his son's life.

You're jumping to conclusions.

Hardly. He hadn't mistaken that flash of Roy Barnes when Nick smiled.

He heard the brittle sound of wood cracking as the frame separated in his hand. As he was trying to shove the pieces back together, he spotted another photo. Picking it up, he saw it was a professional photograph of a toddler sitting on a blanket—a much younger version of Nick. He wore a T-shirt and overalls and was holding a large ball.

Walker started to set it down, then hesitated. The details were fuzzy in his mind, but the picture looked eerily similar to one his mother had of him.

Probably taken by the same photographer. How many could there be in this tiny town?

He started to slide the photo out of its frame, but heard footsteps in the next room. He shoved it back onto the shelf and moved away just before Jen appeared, followed by Nick. As she paused to set a timer on the dining-room table, Nick tried to move around her.

Jen's jeans had holes in the knees, and her baggy green sweatshirt said UW Milwaukee. Her face was pale. "Walker." She rubbed her arms as if she was cold. "What are you doing here?"

"Mom!" Nick interrupted. "Do you know who this is? It's Walker Barnes. He's—"

"I know who he is," she said as she touched the boy's arm. "Go downstairs and help Grandma with the laundry. Then start your homework."

The kid flushed. "You can't send me away like I'm a baby or something. I'm—"

"Nick. Downstairs. Now."

The boy stared at her for a long moment. Then, with a quick look at Walker, he ran down the stairs. A door slammed moments later.

"What do you want?" Jen's gaze darted around the room. She nudged the baseball equipment to the side with her foot, and when one ball got away from her, she snatched it up.

"How old is Nick, Jen?"

"Nick? He's fifteen. Why?" she asked with a puzzled frown.

Fifteen.

It had been almost sixteen years since Jen had led him into that janitor's closet at the high school. Those few minutes had changed his life forever. Had they also created Nick?

Walker took a step toward her, then stopped himself before he put his hands on her. "Is he mine?"

She frowned. "What? What are you talking about?"

"Nick," he said, struggling to keep his voice down. "Is he my son?"

She stared at him for a moment as if she hadn't understood the question, then the baseball fell from her hand, bounced off the table and rolled across the floor. "No! He's not your son!"

Color leached out of her face as he watched her. Was she really that surprised? She hadn't even thought it was a possibility? Or had she merely chosen to believe that Tony was the father? At that point, Tony's prospects had been a hell of a lot better than his. Walker carried the constant stink of a fishing boat on his skin. Tony was headed to the major leagues as a hot pitching prospect.

Tony had been a much better bet as a provider.

"Are you sure?"

"*Am I sure?* Are you crazy? Of course I am."

"When is his birthday?"

She glanced at the stairs to the basement, then hurried to the front door. "Out here. I don't want Nick or my mother to overhear any of this ridiculous conversation."

Practically pushing Walker out, she followed him onto the enclosed porch and shut the door, then folded her arms.

"When's his birthday?"

"None of your business."

"Maybe it is."

She flung the storm door open. "Get out of here, Walker. Is this why you stuck around? You didn't have enough fun tormenting me at the wedding? You wanted to dig a little deeper?"

"You think I was tormenting you on Saturday?" He leaned closer and felt a kick of satisfaction when she flinched away. "You haven't seen anything. If Nick is mine, I'm not going to let it go like I did the last time you screwed me. I'm not going to cover up for you like I did in high school. If he's my son, I'll make sure everyone knows. Including Nick."

She sucked in a breath. Then she shoved him backward. Hard. "Don't you dare threaten my son, Walker. *My* son. And Tony's. If this is your idea of a joke, you're disgusting. Get out of my house and never come back."

She tried to slam the storm door on him, but he grabbed the handle and held on. "When is his birthday, Jen?"

She turned and ran into the house, and he let the outer door slam as he followed her. Before he could step into the house, she reappeared with the baseball bat.

"We're done talking." Holding the bat on her shoulder, she blocked the entrance, guarding her house. Her family. "Go."

"We're not done with this, Jen."

"Oh, yes, we are."

If he took a step closer, she'd swing that bat at his head. He knew it.

Losing his temper had been a mistake. He hadn't thought about Jen in years. When he'd run into her at the wedding, he'd had some fun with her. But after seeing Nick, all the fun had vanished, replaced by anger. "Maybe I jumped to conclusions."

"You think?" She moved her hands on the handle of the bat, and he took a step backward. "Get out, Walker."

"I'm not going to forget about this."

"Neither am I."

Pulling the storm door closed behind him, he

watched her in the wavy glass as he backed down the steps. When he reached the sidewalk, she slammed the inner door. Even from outside, he could hear the lock engage.

JEN SLUMPED ONTO THE COUCH and let the bat fall to the floor. Oh, my God. Where had he gotten that idea?

She reached for a throw pillow and clutched it to her chest. Even through the heavy fabric and stuffing, her heart thundered against her hands. She closed her eyes to hold back the nausea.

"What the hell were you doing?" Nick yelled from the doorway to the basement.

The pillow dropped to the floor as she jumped to her feet. "I told you to stay downstairs." Had he heard any of the conversation?

"I heard yelling. I saw you swinging that bat at Walker's head. What is the matter with you?"

"I did not swing at him." She would have, though. She wouldn't have hesitated if he tried to get through her to Nick. "He just needed a little incentive to leave."

"Mom! Are you out of your frigging mind?" Nick shoved his hands through his hair, leaving it sticking out. "Do you have any idea who that is?"

"Of course I do." She picked up the bat and set it carefully with the rest of Tommy's equipment.

"Walker Barnes! At my house! And my crazy mother takes a baseball bat to him." He yanked open the door and ran across the porch to the storm door, peering outside. "Where did he go?"

"Back to where he came from, I hope." She pressed her hands to her hot cheeks. "Why do you care? And how do you know who he is?"

"Why do I care?" He swung around to face her, and she saw tears glistening in his eyes. "Walker *frigging* Barnes. The owner of GeekBoy. The genius who designed my favorite video games. He was *in my house,* and you chased him away with a baseball bat."

"Wait. What do you mean, he *owns* GeekBoy?" He'd told Tony he wrote video games.

"He started it ages ago. After his first game hit big," Nick said impatiently.

GeekBoy. Her stomach rolled. That was a huge company. They had a big display of games in every electronics store. She should know—she'd bought most of them for Nick.

Walker would have buckets of money. She couldn't just dismiss him as a crazy man. Money meant lawyers. Questions. Publicity. It wouldn't matter that he was wrong. Everyone would find out what he thought. Including Nick and Tony.

"Are you sure that's who he was?"

"His picture is on GeekBoy's Web site," Nick said. He rolled his eyes as if she was an idiot for not knowing. "He's in all the magazines. I was going to ask him about his newest game, but now he'll never want to talk to me." He punched the wall. "God! He'll think I'm a total freak. Way to go, Mom."

Tommy came running into the room. "What's going on? Why are you yelling?"

"The guy who owns GeekBoy was here." Nick turned to his brother. "And Mom swung your baseball bat at him. Like she was gonna knock his head off."

"Whoa." He picked up the bat and looked it over. "Dude, that's major."

Jen rubbed her suddenly pounding temples. The next time Nick told the story, she would have sent Walker's head rolling down the front steps. "Settle down. Both of you. Nick, stay away from Walker. You are not to go looking for him. Are you clear on that?"

He stared at her, mutinous, his face flushed.

"Nick?"

"No, I'm not clear on that. I *hate* you. You ruin *everything*." He ran down the steps. The floor beneath her shook when he slammed his bedroom door in the basement.

"He's really mad," Tommy said after a moment.

"He'll get over it." She hoped.

"I don't know." Tommy turned to her, and she read his accusation. "He, like, worships that guy. Nick talks about him all the time, about how he's going to write video games, too." He shook his head. "Sucks to be you, Mom."

He went downstairs and she heard him saying something to Nick through the door.

At least she'd managed to unite her boys. Against her.

She fell onto the couch, curled into a ball and wrapped her arms around herself. She couldn't stop shivering. Why would he suddenly want to be a parent to a boy he didn't know?

How could he think he was Nick's father? What reason could he have?

She'd been careful. They'd used a condom. Nick was *Tony's* son.

Wasn't he?

Yes. It had never occurred to her that Walker might have made her pregnant. It couldn't be true. He was just trying to get even with her for what she'd done in high school.

Would he talk to Nick? God, no. *Don't let him do that to my baby.* Don't let a few casual words bring Nick's world crashing down.

The Walker she remembered wouldn't let this go. In high school, he'd asked a million questions in class. When he got his teeth into a problem, he wouldn't give up until he'd solved it.

If he really believed Nick was his son, he'd be relentless.

No. He was just playing with her. Punishing her. He'd certainly enjoyed tormenting her at the wedding.

She took a deep, shuddering breath and tossed the pillow on the floor. If he was only trying to make her suffer, she could survive. She'd become an expert at surviving.

He would have to leave town eventually. According to Nick, Walker had a company to run.

As she replaced the pillow on the couch and picked up Tommy's baseball equipment, the smell of something burning drifted out of her kitchen.

The duck. Her test recipe.

Smoke billowed from the oven when she opened the door and pulled out a blackened, shrunken bird. She tossed it in the sink. The perfect way to wrap up her day.

WALKER'S PORSCHE ROCKED as he slammed on the brakes in the parking lot of the tiny county park. As soon as he turned off the engine, he heard the rhythmic sound of waves rolling onto the shore. He shoved his hands into his pockets and stepped onto the grassy strip between asphalt and sand. Ten steps took him to the beach.

His shoes filled with sand as he headed toward the water, shivering against the sharp wind blowing off the lake. He wasn't dressed for the beach in April.

The water was a sullen, choppy gray. Whitecaps broke away from the shore, then curled onto the beach. A piece of driftwood tumbled in with the next wave, dripping with green strands of seaweed. He picked it up and hurled it as far as he could into the lake. He spotted another piece farther down and threw that one, too.

He'd handled it all wrong. Handled Jen all wrong. Of course she'd chased him out of her house. The palm-size rock he threw landed with a splash. He'd told her he was going to fight her for her son.

He'd been too angry to think rationally. Her son—Nick—wasn't a commodity. A toy to be passed around, played with, then handed back. Did he really want to be a father? To take on the responsibility of a teenage boy? Or did he just want to punish Jen?

What made him think he could be a father, anyway?

His own father hadn't been such a great role model. Instead of trying to help his son succeed, he'd tried to force him to stay in Otter Tail and take over the fishing boat. Even when he knew Walker hated that life.

Another rock went into the lake. Another piece of driftwood. Walker threw until he couldn't see any more wood on the shore. Until his shoulder burned and ached. Then he dropped onto the cold sand.

He hadn't gotten where he was by letting emotion cloud his thinking. A smart man would gather proof before confronting Jen. Before deciding he wanted to give up his carefree, single lifestyle to be responsible for a teenage boy. A son.

What *would* he do if it turned out Nick was his son?

CHAPTER FIVE

THREE DAYS.

That's how long it had been since the scene at Jen's house, and he hadn't found the pictures of himself as a toddler—the ones he needed as proof that he could be Nick's dad. He hadn't been able to get hold of the woman who'd cleaned out his parents' house and put the contents into storage after his father died. His mother had died five years earlier and he hadn't been back to the house since.

The sun beat down on Walker's back and reflected off the asphalt as he strained to pedal up the last hill before Otter Tail. When he reached the top, he yanked the plastic bottle from its wire holder and squirted a stream of lukewarm water into his mouth.

He'd biked to the edge of exhaustion, but it hadn't erased the image of Nick from his mind. The smile that could have been his father's. His green eyes.

He shoved the water bottle back in place and

kicked off the pavement, dislodging a landslide of tiny pebbles. He'd gone to the Harp every night since that confrontation. She'd been there, working, but she'd managed to avoid him.

Not tonight. He'd acted out of rage when he'd threatened to confront Nick. Something he never did.

Now he had to fix it.

The first houses appeared on the outskirts of town, and he realized he needed to slow down. The bike skidded as he braked, and he struggled to control it while watching for approaching cars. It was only April, but the tourists were arriving. He'd better get Jen out of his head and pay attention, because people took that curve way too fast.

As he rode slowly through town, he pedaled past a park with a baseball field. There was a crowd gathered, and adults were playing. A kid with blond hair, wearing earbuds, leaned against a brown car. Jen's beater.

Nick.

Walker slid to a halt and saw that he was playing a video game. On a handheld GeekBoy.

Walker swallowed, the black-and-red of the console blurring. Why was he so surprised? Why was his heart suddenly pounding? They'd sold millions of those units. He'd seen lots of kids using them before today.

A piece of plastic and metal looked a lot different when it was your own kid with it. Or someone who *might* be your kid, anyway.

What did Nick think of it? Did he like it? Were there things he would change?

You don't know for sure he's your son.

Nick glanced up from the game, and his eyes widened. He yanked out the earbuds. Music with a heavy bass beat blared as they dangled in his fist. "Mr. Barnes! Uh, hi!" He glanced toward the diamond, then wiped his hand on his jeans. "You, uh, remember me?"

"Of course I do." *Play it cool. Casual.* "How do you like the unit?" He nodded at the handheld.

"It rocks. I got it for my birthday."

Walker's hands tightened on his handlebars. They'd just released that model the previous Christmas. "Yeah? So how long have you had it?"

"Since February."

February. That would have been almost nine months after Jen's little seduction scene.

"Uh, are you okay?" Nick was shifting his gaze between Walker and the baseball diamond.

"I'm fine." The bike was suddenly too heavy, and he dropped it onto the grass. "A little shaky and sweaty right now."

"I mean about the other day," Nick said in a rush.

"My mom was scary, man. She didn't mean anything she said. You know? She gets weird sometimes."

"Did you…hear everything we said?"

"Well, no. But I saw her with the bat. Wow."

"It's okay. That was between your mom and me." He noticed the boy's running gear, and nodded at the baseball diamond. "Are you playing ball?"

Nick reddened. "No, that's my mom's deal. But she, uh, likes it when I come to her games."

Walker followed his gaze and saw Jen, wearing baggy shorts and a faded black T-shirt, pitching to an overweight man at the plate.

She threw the ball in a smooth motion, the stretch of her body emphasizing her sleek muscles, and the man at the plate spun around as he tried to hit it. Jen had pitched for the softball team in high school. It looked as if she was still pretty good.

"It's nice of you to support her." Walker struggled to keep from smiling. He wasn't so far removed from his teenage years to know that a kid Nick's age would rather die than come to his mother's baseball game voluntarily. "So does she play often?"

"Every Saturday morning."

The man at the plate had struck out, and a woman was up to bat. She hit a ball that dribbled toward second base, and the man trying to field it bobbled it awkwardly. Jen yelled something at him, then turned to face the next batter. Her T-shirt was damp, and it clung to her curves. "Nobody else on the team looks as if they know what they're doing."

Nick snorted. "They don't." He shoved the mp3 player into his pocket and watched the game for a moment, a tiny smile on his face.

"Mom calls this the penalty box for baseball parents. Anyone who yells at a kid or the ump at one of the games she coaches has to sign up for this team. If they don't, their kid can't be on her team anymore. She got all the other coaches to do it, too."

From the fierce satisfaction on Nick's face, Walker guessed he'd been yelled at while playing baseball. "Interesting idea."

"It only takes a couple of games for them to apologize," Nick said. "They find out fast it's not as easy as it looks."

"You a baseball player? GeekBoy is developing a game. I could get you a copy, if you like."

Walker glanced at the field, but Jen apparently hadn't noticed him talking to Nick. She'd be furious if she did, but she was already furious with him. He was willing to risk her anger to talk to Nick for a few minutes.

"A new game? Sweet." Nick stared at the field for another moment, and Walker saw the loathing on his face. "I'll try it out, but I hate baseball."

"Why's that? Didn't your father play baseball?"

Nick clenched his jaw. "Yeah, he did. And he thinks everyone should love it just as much as he does." He kicked a small rock in the road. "Baseball is for losers. Trying to hit a little ball with a piece of wood is stupid. Standing in the sun, waiting for a ball to come to you, sucks the big one. I like computers better."

"Yeah, I'm pretty fond of them myself." Nick's shoulders relaxed and he grinned. "What kinds of stuff do you like to do on the computer?"

Words spilled out of Nick's mouth. *C++*. *Java*. *Visual Basic*. All programming buzzwords. Walker wondered if Nick was trying to create his own games.

"You're doing some complicated stuff."

The kid actually blushed. "My computer is pretty old, but I do okay." He swallowed. "Mr. Barnes, can I ask you something?"

"Sure." Walker tensed. What could he want?

"Do you have a release date for *Sorceress* yet?"

Ah, that he could answer. "Not yet." He gave Nick the standard response he gave to reporters and columnists. There were still some kinks to be worked out, and this game had to kill for GeekBoy. He'd gambled a lot of money on it.

Then a thought struck Walker. He'd found the perfect excuse to stick around Otter Tail. "I'll be testing a beta version at the Harp while I'm here. To work out the wrinkles."

"No way!" Dropping all pretense of coolness, Nick tossed his game console through the car's open window. "When? I'll be there. I'll bring a couple of my buddies, too. We'll be, like, your early adopters."

"I'll let you know when we do it." All he had to do was get Quinn to agree.

"That's so hot." The teen frowned at the baseball players, who were gathered in the center of the field. "That game better be over. I need to tell Dave and Stevie about this."

As Nick spoke, Walker spotted Jen striding toward them. A streak of mud smeared one of her socks and half her hair had fallen out of her ponytail. The sports bag slung over her shoulder swayed in time with her stride.

Her cheeks were flushed. Her eyes pinned him to the car, and she clenched her hands.

She shoved her hair behind her ear.

"Nick. What's going on?"

"I was discussing games with Mr. Barnes. He's going to demo *Sorceress* at the Harp."

"What's *Sorceress?*"

"God, Mom, don't you know *anything*? Geek-Boy has a new game coming out, and he's going to run it at the Harp. Beta test it. That's, like, huge."

"Is that right?" She stared at her son for a moment, and he held her gaze defiantly. "I'm disappointed with you, Nick, and you know why. Go get Tommy so we can leave."

"Mom! He stopped to talk to me."

"I don't care. Go."

Nick rolled his eyes at Walker, as if inviting him into the "she's such a loser" club. He strolled toward the playground, taking his time. Jen watched him, her lips tightening, then turned to Walker.

"I told you to stay away from my son. I'm calling the police."

She dropped the sports bag to the ground, and he heard the hollow sound of wood jostling together. Bats.

He had to remember to not be around her if she had a bat nearby.

When she reached into the bag, he put his palm on her arm to stop her. "Hold on, Jen.

She jerked away from him. "Keep your hands to yourself, Walker."

She tried to step around him, but he blocked her path. "I need to apologize. I'm sorry. I was completely out of line the other day."

She stared at him for a long moment. Jen had always been smart. "Fine. You've apologized. Now leave before Nick and Tommy get here."

"I was wrong to threaten you. I lost my temper." The memory made him grind his teeth. He hardly ever lost control. "I won't do it again."

"I don't care how many times you lose your temper. We won't be around to see it."

"God, you're tough."

"You have no idea."

He shoved a hand through his still-damp hair. "Look, Jen, I want to start over. Forget what happened the other day."

"Are you kidding me? I'm supposed to forget that you came to my house, accused me of hiding your child and threatened to tell him you were his father?" She put her fists on her hips. "You think you can charm me stupid? Not a chance."

"I never thought I could."

"Then what do you want?"

"I want to find out if Nick is my son. A chance to get to know him if he is."

"You're out of your mind. He's not yours."

"I need to know that for sure."

"I know who fathered my child!"

A bead of sweat trickled down her temple, and she wiped it off with the bottom of her T-shirt, revealing a pale crescent of flat belly. Her arm was tanned next to the milky skin of her abdomen, and another drop of sweat rolled down her side.

He couldn't tear his gaze away.

She hastily dropped her shirt into place.

"I know his birthday is in February."

She paled. "Just because you have enough money to find out anything you want doesn't give you the right to pry into our lives. What difference does it make when his birthday is?"

"You're good at math. I know, because we were in the same classes. Count it out."

"Once, Walker." She glanced over her shoulder, clearly looking for her kids. "We had sex once. We used a condom. End of discussion."

"Condoms fail. And my luck was really crappy that particular day."

Her cheeks reddened. "Luck had nothing to do with it. Sorry to wreck your tidy little revenge plans, but he's not yours. Tony and I were having sex. A lot."

"Are you willing to get a DNA test?"

"No!" She stared at him, appalled. "You're out of your mind. Nick's a bright kid. He'll figure out why you're doing it." She grabbed the bag from the ground and tried to throw it into the open window of the car. It slid down and landed in the gutter. "It would change our relationship forever. And his relationship with Tony."

"I can get a court order."

"I doubt it. You have no grounds." She snatched up the bag. "I'd deny anything happened."

"You'd lie under oath?

"To protect my son? Absolutely."

"Are you daring me to take you to court?"

She drew a deep breath, and he had a flash of her wearing that low-cut black dress at the wedding.

"I'm not giving him a DNA test."

"I'll ask Tony for permission, then."

She paled again, and the tiny freckles on her nose looked like spots of dark paint. "Don't you dare go to Tony. Don't involve him in your craziness."

"Then agree to the test. Nick doesn't need to know. Get me some hairs from his brush."

She glanced at the playground. Nick was leaning against the slide, talking to Tommy.

"What is *wrong* with you? Don't you have enough going on in your life? Why are you harassing me?"

"Because there's a chance he's mine. And I'm not going away until I find out."

"Then I guess you're going to be in Otter Tail for a long time."

"If you don't want to get Tony involved, then it's up to you. But I'm going to get to know Nick. And sooner or later, there will be a DNA test."

If he spent enough time with him, Walker would know, wouldn't he? He'd be able to tell if the kid was his son.

"Why do you think he's yours? Other than his birthday?"

That moment from the wedding replayed in Walker's head, as it had done a hundred times already. A young Roy Barnes grinning at him. "He looks like my dad."

"What?"

"I saw him smile. He looked just like my father."

"You're delusional. He looks like my mom. Their baby pictures are identical."

"You don't think it's a little too coincidental that he's into computers?"

She made a scoffing sound. "Most kids his age play computer games."

"Do they try to write them?"

"Nick's not doing that."

"Do you know what he's doing with the computer?"

"No. He tries to explain it, but I don't understand what he's talking about. I'd understand if he said he was writing games."

She leaned against the car and yanked off her baseball spikes and socks. She threw them into the bag and pulled out a pair of flip-flops. The tiny pink-and-yellow flowers on the straps were vivid next to her pale skin. Her toenails were painted bright red, and she curled them into the green shoes. When he looked up, she was watching him.

Her chest beneath the damp T-shirt rose and fell a little too fast.

"While I'm getting to know Nick, I'll find some pictures of myself as a baby. We can compare them to yours. If they look alike, will you agree to the DNA test?"

"No. Why do you need him to be your son?"

"You don't think I have the right to know if I have a child? To have some say in his life?" Was he trying to change history? Trying to be a different father than Roy Barnes? Maybe. But he would make sure any child of his could follow his own dreams.

"A lot of babies look alike, Walker."

"Yes or no, Jen. If the pictures match will you agree to the test? Since you're so sure it will be negative, what do you have to lose?" In the distance, he saw Nick and Tommy trudging across the grass.

She picked up the gym bag and stuffed it through the open window. "He's not your son, Walker. Now get out of here before they get back to the car."

CHAPTER SIX

"No, WE DON'T HAVE any arugula." Jen flipped two burgers and a chicken breast a little too hard. "Isn't it kind of early for the tourists?"

"You're touchy tonight." Maddie leaned against the counter and watched her shrewdly. "Would it have anything to do with Walker Barnes?"

"Who?"

Her friend laughed and headed for the door. "He's still asking about you. I thought you guys might hit it off. He's perfect for you."

"In what universe would that be?" Jen shoved the spatula under one of the burgers and it flew off the grill and onto the floor.

"The one where you're so flustered when I say his name that you drop food."

"Knock it off, Maddie." She tossed the burger into the trash and slapped another frozen patty on the grill.

"He's going to be here awhile. He asked Quinn if he could demo his new game in the pub."

"Yeah? When's he doing that?" She held her breath, waiting for Maddie's answer.

"In about a month," her friend said airily.

"A *month*?" She dropped her spatula. "How long does it take to throw a game into a console and put it on a screen?"

"He said he's got some work to do before it'll be ready."

She couldn't work here for another month with Walker hanging around every night. Maybe Pat at the bank would give her the loan for her restaurant now if she agreed to a higher interest rate. She could save some money if she bought used kitchen equipment. She'd have Nick search eBay and Craigslist for what she wanted.

Walker's presence in Otter Tail was turning out to be a good thing. The nudge in the back she needed.

No. There was nothing that would make Walker's presence palatable.

Jen could feel Maddie's gaze on her, but she pretended to be busy at the stove. "Why don't you get to know him?" her friend finally said. "Go on a date. You remember those, don't you?"

A date with Walker. Right. "Just because you drank the happily-ever-after Kool-Aid doesn't mean the rest of us want to." She plated slices of meat loaf and garlic mashed potatoes, then slid the two meals onto the stainless-steel table.

"What's wrong with him?" Maddie put the food on her tray. "He's good-looking, fun, smart. Rich. What's not to like?"

"Deliver the specials before they get cold, Mrs. Murphy."

That distracted Maddie, as Jen had known it would. "Don't call me that. Maddie Murphy sounds like a soap-opera actress."

"It's your name, isn't it?"

"I didn't change my name and you know it." Maddie lifted the tray. "Maybe after we have kids."

She backed through the swinging door. "We're not done with this conversation," she called as she disappeared into the noisy pub.

"Oh, yes, we are," Jen muttered.

Unbidden, she thought about that moment on the baseball field when she'd caught Walker staring at her after she'd changed her shoes. For an instant, she'd imagined desire in his clear green eyes. And her treacherous body had responded.

That's what happened when you lived like a nun.

But it hadn't been just some random guy who'd stirred her desire. It had been Walker's butt in those biking shorts. Walker's muscles beneath the jersey. Walker's scent.

How pathetic was that? He'd laugh his ass off if he knew. Then he'd figure out how to use it against her. How to use it to make her agree to a DNA test.

That could never happen. Nick and Tony already had a tenuous relationship. They fought over sports, over Nick's time on the computer, over his friends.

Nick had a serious case of hero worship for Walker. If he had any idea what Walker was thinking, it would irreparably damage his relationship with Tony.

And Tony. He didn't know she'd actually had sex with Walker. If he found out, he wouldn't let it go. Every time they fought about anything, he'd throw it in her face.

Hypocritical wasn't in her ex-husband's vocabulary.

As she was about to slide the burger and another chicken breast off the grill, Jorge, the dishwasher, yelled, *"Mierda!"*

A blast of water hit Jen in the back. She yelped and spun around to see Jorge holding the hose attached to the sink. It writhed like a snake, spewing water in all directions. "Turn off the water!" she called.

By the time he got it off, she and Jorge were both soaked. He had somehow managed to kink the hose, and it had sprung a leak.

Jen swiped her wet hair out of her face. "Get the mop and clean this up," she told the young man. "And don't look so worried," she added, softening her voice. "It was an accident. It'll be fine."

The swinging door to the pub opened and Walker stepped in. "Jen? You okay?"

She shoved her dripping ponytail over her shoulder and it landed with a wet slap. "Just peachy." She reached for a sponge and crouched next to the grill. "Patrons aren't allowed in the kitchen."

Walker took the mop and bucket from Jorge and said something to him in Spanish. The young man's shoulders relaxed and he returned to the sink.

"What are you doing?" Jen asked Walker.

"Cleaning up the mess." He swabbed the floor as if he knew what he was doing, wringing out the mop and moving on to another section before she could object. His biceps bunched and flexed, and the T-shirt he wore pulled taut across his chest as he worked.

She shook her head and let the sponge soak up some water. It was a pitifully small amount, but she walked gingerly across the wet floor and squeezed it into the bucket.

As she headed back to the grill, Walker barred her way. "Let me get it. You'll be here all night with that sponge."

"Don't be ridiculous. Jorge and I can clean it up. Get out of here." She made shooing motions with her hands, but he continued to mop.

"Jorge needs to dry all those dishes. You have food cooking."

The burger and chicken were smoking. She dumped them into the garbage, then threw fresh ones onto the grill. She'd wasted a lot of food tonight.

"Where did you learn to mop like that?" she asked as she watched Walker.

He pushed down on the wringer hard enough to make water squirt into the air. "My father had a fishing boat."

Had she known Walker's father was a fisherman? Had she bothered to find out anything about him, other than his skill with a computer, before she had sex with him?

She reached blindly for plates and buns. So much pain, so many consequences for one stupid, thoughtless act. Tony had lost the career he'd wanted so badly, Walker had lost his scholarship and Jen had lost her self-respect.

Maddie stuck her head through the door. "Those are the last two orders," she called. She glanced at the walls, still dripping water, and the bucket in the middle of the floor. "What happened?"

"Minor leak," Walker answered.

"What are you doing back here?"

"Cleaning it up. I was walking past the kitchen when all hose broke loose."

Jen rolled her eyes. "That's lame, Barnes."

"Programmers don't have a sense of humor. It's part of the job description."

The door closed behind Maddie, but not before Jen saw her friend's smug smile.

"We appreciate the help," Jen said. "But I'll finish."

"You can take over when you're done cooking." He wrung out the mop once more, then grabbed her sponge and began to wipe the walls. By the time she'd plated the two orders and shut down the grill, he'd dried the room.

"Thank you, Walker," she said as she began her closing routine. "Tell Quinn he owes you a couple of beers."

"Are you going to have one with me?"

"Sure," she said easily. "I'll meet you up front."

"I'll wait and help Jorge."

"You don't have to do that. I'll be out in a few minutes."

He tossed the sponge in the bucket and wandered over to the dishwasher. "I haven't fallen for that kind of line since…"

He paused, and she glanced at him. His expression was easy to read. *Since you asked me to change Tony's grade.*

She pushed harder at the metal blade she used to scrape the grill. He was right. She'd planned to sneak out the back door again.

Jorge was working on his last load of dishes when she wrapped up, and Walker was leaning against the wall. Waiting for her. She grabbed her jacket and purse from the hook at the rear of the kitchen, then paused. If she slipped out the back, Walker would just follow her. The best strategy would be to go out the front and lose him in the crowd.

She tried to walk through the swinging doors, but Walker caught her arm and leaned close. Too close. "If you try to leave, I'll tell Maddie I've asked you on a date and you refused."

Her friend would hound her mercilessly. She'd dig for details. Jen couldn't bear the constant reminder of what she'd done to Walker so long ago.

"That's a lie." His hand was warm on her arm, his fingers slightly callused. She let his warmth sink into her muscles, her bones, for a long instant before she pulled away.

"Go out to dinner with me," he said promptly.

"No!"

"There. I'd be telling her the truth."

Two could play this game. He was trying to throw her off balance. Since Jen was quite sure he was no more interested in her than she was in him, she'd go along with him. Turn the tables and make him think she was pursuing him.

Then she'd watch *him* squirm.

Looping her arm through his, she smiled to herself at his surprise. "Let's go have that beer."

WALKER GLANCED AT JEN as they stepped into the noisy crowd. What was going on?

One minute he'd been needling her, and the next she was acting all chummy. As if she actually wanted to have a drink with him.

He knew she'd been planning on bolting out the back door. He'd seen her eyeing it. Now she slid onto one of the stools at the bar and smiled at Quinn.

"I'll have a Leinie, boss."

"Me, too," Walker said.

Quinn glanced at the two of them, and Jen edged closer to Walker. Beneath the smell of beer and grilled onions in the air, he caught the tang of lemon in her hair. When he leaned a little toward her, the subtle scent of her skin drifted over him.

"Here you go." Quinn set the two beers on the

marble bar and smiled. "You want some company or do you want to be alone?"

Instead of bristling at the implication, Jen smiled back. "Hard to be alone in a room full of people."

What the hell was she up to?

Quinn grinned. "I'll let you two figure out the logistics." He moved away from them.

"What are you doing?" Walker demanded.

She lifted the glass of beer and took a drink. "Having a beer," she said, setting it on the coaster. "What does it look like?"

This was about Nick, and about convincing Jen to let him do a DNA test. Walker had figured if he irritated her enough, she'd give in just to get rid of him.

Instead, he was sitting on a bar stool too close to her, drinking a suddenly tasteless Leinie.

"Tell me about Nick," he asked.

Her hand tightened on the glass, but she said, "What do you want to know?"

He wasn't even sure what questions to ask about kids. "Um, whatever you want to tell me."

Her smile was amused, as if she'd read his mind. It faded as she centered her glass in front of her. "He's a typical teen. Always testing the limits," she said quietly. "But a good kid. He doesn't like sports, but that's Tony's fault. He pushed too hard, and Nick finally rebelled."

"He likes computers."

"He loves computers. He'd spend all day and all night on his, if I let him."

Walker absorbed the information and realized it wasn't nearly enough. The same things could be said about hundreds of boys Nick's age. Walker wanted to know what was beneath the surface.

What kind of person he was.

What parts of Nick might have come from Walker.

He wanted to look at Nick and see himself.

And wasn't that a kick in the ass? He'd never thought about having kids. Never even considered it.

Not even with his ex-fiancée. They hadn't talked about children. And now he hungered for information about a boy he'd never even known about.

Jen finished her beer and stood. "Thanks for the drink, Walker. I have to get going."

He slid off his stool. "I'll walk you to your car."

"I didn't drive." He saw the instant she realized the trap. "So sit back down and enjoy your beer."

"I'll take you home." He finished the last of it. "We're having so much fun, I don't want the evening to end."

CHAPTER SEVEN

"It has been fun," she said easily, "but I don't want a ride home. I like to walk after I work." She shrugged on her jacket and began to weave her way through the crowd.

He threw a bill on the bar, watching as she waved at someone in the band. The woman playing drums waved a stick back at her and the guitar players nodded. Then Jen pushed through the door and disappeared.

Walker grabbed his jacket off the hook on the wall and followed her. She was already half a block ahead of him.

She'd shoved her hands into her pockets. As he came up behind her, she looked over her hunched shoulder.

"Walker. What are you doing?"

"Walking you home, since you don't want a ride."

"I've been finding my way home for a long time."

"Then I'll just keep you company." He edged a little closer. "Looks like you're cold."

Her shoulders relaxed and she took her hands out of her pockets. "I'm fine."

The air was crisp and chilly, a typical late April evening in northern Wisconsin. A few clouds scudded across the sky, and millions of stars twinkled above them. He'd forgotten about the nights up here. A person could breathe beneath a sky like that.

"Go back to the pub, Walker. You can harass me all you want, but I won't agree to a DNA test."

"How about the pictures? Will you look at them?"

"Fine." She stopped. "Let me see them."

"I don't have them yet."

She resumed walking. "Talk to me when you do."

"Nick is going to find me, you know. He wants to talk gaming with me. It would be easier if you didn't forbid him to spend time with me."

"Easier for who? You? It's not my job to simplify your life."

"Easier for Nick. Do you want him sneaking around?"

"He wouldn't do that." But there was no conviction in her voice.

"It doesn't take a genius to guess that he will."

"You don't know my son, Walker."

"I understand fifteen-year-old boys. I used to be one."

"I'll think about it."

"Good." He smiled to himself. Her first concession. There would be more. The first one was always the hardest to get.

She crossed the street without looking at him. "Go back to the Harp. I'm not going to cave because you're following me home." She glanced at him out of the corner of her eye. "I don't like being pressured. You push me, I'll push back."

"I'll consider myself warned. Why don't you tell me about yourself while we walk home?"

"There's nothing I'm interested in sharing."

"Really? Not one single detail?" She looked at him, and beneath the wariness, he thought he saw anticipation. Was she attracted to him?

"No. And why would you care?"

"You're the mother of my son. Of course I want to find out who you are."

She clenched the strap of her purse. "No, I'm not."

Could he make her more nervous? Nervous people sometimes blurted out things they hadn't meant to say.

He shortened the distance between them. The

pulse jumped in her throat, and he watched, fascinated. They were so close to the stores that the dark windows of the flower shop they were passing reflected her pale skin and huge eyes.

The sleeves of their coats brushed with a whisper of sound. She moved sideways.

"Careful." He took her arm and steered her past a flowerpot in front of the bookstore. "Don't want you to trip."

She pulled away from him. "Thanks. I know my way around Otter Tail." But she spoiled the effect by stumbling on a crooked piece of the sidewalk.

"Something bothering you?"

She nudged him with her elbow until there was air between them. "Other than a psycho jerk threatening to tell Nick he's really not Tony's son, you mean?"

Grinning, Walker slipped his arm through hers. When she tried to pull away, he pressed her elbow against his side. "I don't want you to stumble again."

"Let go of me, Walker." She wrenched her arm out of his and swung around to face him. "I've had my fill of this."

Behind her, he saw movement at the other end of an alley. Three figures ran past, glancing toward them before they disappeared. One faltered, then recovered and kept going.

Nick. Walker stared down the alley. What was he doing out at this time of night?

And did Jen know he wasn't at home?

Walker would bet any amount of money she didn't. She'd just told him Nick wouldn't sneak around.

A responsible person would tell Jen her son was out late at night.

According to Jen, Walker wasn't responsible for Nick.

Jen had taken advantage of his hesitation and moved several steps ahead. He smiled when he saw her arms plastered to the sides of her body. It looked as if she didn't want to be touched again.

"I'm just making conversation."

"If you wanted conversation, you should have stayed at the Harp. There were plenty of people who wanted to talk to you," she said.

"No, they didn't. They wanted to talk to the owner of GeekBoy. Hoping I'd buy their drinks."

"That's really cynical." She glanced at him. "People in Otter Tail aren't like that."

He shrugged. "Everyone is. It doesn't bother me anymore." He expected it now—he'd seen calculation on too many faces in the past several years.

She slowed. "You must have some real friends. People who don't want anything from you."

"Of course I do. Quinn. I came up here for his wedding, didn't I? And Kirit Patel. He's GeekBoy's vice president. We met when I was a hungry wannabe. Before I sold my first game."

There was silence. "Is that all?" she finally asked.

"Of course not. What do you want? A written list?"

"That's really sad," she said softly. "I don't know what I'd do without my friends."

She sounded as if she felt sorry for him. Him. Millionaire success story.

He had the perfect life—a job he loved and enough money to do whatever he wanted. How had she managed to put him on the defensive? It was none of her business how he lived his life.

They were on Parkside now, where her parents' house was located. He'd be damned if he'd take pity from Jen Summers.

"Do you really think I have such a lonely life?" He grabbed her wrist to stop her, then slid his hand lower, until their palms pressed together. Her hand was a little dry, as if she'd washed it too often.

She jerked away, but not before he felt her fingers tremble.

"You're the one who said 'lonely.' Not me."

He'd been alone most of his life, even when he was growing up. His mother had been bewildered by him. His father had been interested in Walker only as an extension of himself. Someone to continue the family fishing business.

"Quiet isn't lonely. I need calm when I design my games."

"Okay. Your life is exactly the way you want it." She darted a look at him, and he had no trouble reading her expression. *Except in this. You don't control me. Or Nick.*

As if he'd conjured him out of the air, a figure darted across the street behind Jen, headed for the house. Nick. Was he planning on walking in the door right in front of his mother?

Jen began to turn, and Walker tugged her arm. He had to delay her. "How about you? Are you happy?"

"My life is perfect."

"So there's nothing missing?"

"Nothing I can't live without."

Nick was creeping around the side of the house, watching them until he disappeared from sight. If Jen went in now, she'd discover him.

Walker drew her closer. He was just supplying cover for Nick. That's all.

Then she put her hands on his chest, and he forgot all about Nick.

WHAT WAS HE DOING? As Walker pulled her to him, Jen put her hands on his jacket to shove him away. The smell of leather surrounded her. She'd always been a sucker for leather.

His heat burned into her, even through the thick coat. *Move. Now.*

But she didn't move. Neither did he.

He stared down at her, and she couldn't look away. She pushed at him, but her heart wasn't in it.

"This isn't…" He swallowed. "It's not…"

"No. It isn't." She pushed again. "Get away from me."

"*You* get away from *me*. I don't want you," he muttered.

"I don't want you, either." She dropped her hands and tried to step back, but he grabbed them and put them back on his chest, covering them with his. Pressing her fingers into him.

He shook his head, as if to clear it. Then one corner of his mouth lifted. "What the hell."

When his lips met hers, warm and firm and tasting faintly of bitter Lienie, she froze.

But when he touched the seam of her lips with his tongue, stroking gently, desire stirred. And when he nipped her bottom lip, then soothed it, all the passion she hadn't felt for the past two years washed over her in a huge wave. Drowning her in need. In want. She threw her arms around his neck and opened her mouth to him.

Walker shuddered. He wasn't the whip-lean boy she'd held so long ago. Now his chest was hard with muscle and his legs were strong against hers. His hands roamed her back restlessly, stroking her from her neck to her hips, gliding over her curves. He lingered on her right hip, just below her waist. Did he remember the tiny tattoo of the sun and moon he'd found so fascinating?

Memories exploded in her head. The way he'd tasted back then, like spearmint chewing gum. The way he'd touched her, as if she was infinitely precious. The care he'd taken with her, the sweetness that she'd never felt before or since.

The way her muscles had turned to jelly when he'd kissed her.

He urged her backward until her shoulders touched a tree, the bark bumpy against her spine. Then he slid a leg between hers and cupped her face in his hands, still kissing her.

His fingers tangled in her hair and her ponytail holder went flying. Then he buried his face in the heavy mass of it over her neck, inhaling deeply. She turned her head blindly, wanting his mouth on hers again.

She was burrowing beneath his jacket, desperate

to touch his skin, when the headlights of a car flashed past. A horn honked, and someone yelled out the window, "Get a room!"

She shoved him away. He let her go slowly, as if he couldn't bear to stop touching her. Finally, he dropped his hands, breathing as heavily as she was.

They stared at one another for a long moment. Then he thrust his fingers through his hair. "Holy hell."

CHAPTER EIGHT

SHE BACKED AWAY, staring at him, her body still throbbing. "What was that?" she managed to say.

His eyes were dark and shadowed and he breathed too fast. But he shrugged. "Last time I checked, it was called a kiss."

Right. Mr. Cool. "If you think you can seduce me into giving you what you want, forget it. I'm not that gullible."

"You think that's what I'm doing? Like you seduced me in high school to get what you wanted?"

She sucked in a sharp breath. His barb was well-aimed, and it struck deep. Made it impossible to speak.

"Doesn't feel very good, does it?"

Her stomach churned. "No. It doesn't." She looked at the house, only a few yards away. A refuge. "I'm sorry about what I did. It was horrible and wrong and mean. If I could go back in time and change things, I would. I can't. But I'm not that girl anymore."

He clenched his jaw and slapped the tree. "You skated, didn't you? So what is there for you to regret?"

"You think I got off scot-free?" The pain of her divorce was still a fresh wound, but there was no way she'd tell him what had happened between her and Tony. "I paid a price, too."

He sighed. "It was a kiss, Jen. That's all. It wasn't the first step in my master plan for world domination. I wasn't thinking about…Nick or high school or anything else."

Which meant he was. He'd probably sensed her weakness and pounced. He was the kind of opponent who looked for any opening.

Why had she kissed him back?

She didn't want to think about that. Didn't want to think about the irony of being attracted to Walker. "Fine. Just a kiss. Already forgotten." She wished.

"Right." He looked over her shoulder at the house. "Looks like everyone's sleeping in there."

"They better be."

A tiny smile curled his mouth. "Do you want me to walk you the rest of the way? You look a little…unsettled."

"I can walk up the steps myself," she said,

pleased at the coolness in her voice. "I'm perfectly all right."

She turned and hurried up the stairs to the porch. She felt him watching her.

It took her three tries before she got the key in the lock.

JEN PUSHED AWAY the folder of pictures and the spreadsheet and sipped her coffee. She shuddered. It was cold and too bitter to drink. But it reminded her to add a coffee machine to the growing list of equipment she'd need for her restaurant.

Her maybe-not-that-far-in-the-future restaurant.

She'd been putting every extra penny in her savings account, but it wasn't accumulating very quickly. If she waited until she could get a traditional loan from the bank, she'd be gray and arthritic. Too old to stand at a stove for hours.

No. There was a way to make this happen. Pat Larson at the bank had promised to work with her. Nick was already looking for used equipment online. She was going to talk to Frank Jones about renting his store.

Whatever happened, she was done worrying about seeing Walker at the Harp every night. Knowing him, he'd seek her out. Touch her and make it seem like an accident. Press her for a decision.

She'd stay as far away from him as possible.

Under no circumstances would she kiss him again.

It had been three days, and her heart still quickened when she thought about his body pressed against hers. Desire pooled low in her abdomen when she remembered their kiss.

No, there would be no more kisses under the trees in the moonlight.

Gathering up the papers spread out on the kitchen table, she shoved them in the folder and replaced them in the file cabinet in the dining room.

Sooner or later, she realized with a roll of her stomach, she'd have to let him talk to Nick. Get to know him. There wasn't any alternative, not with his threat to ask Tony for permission to do the DNA testing. That was out of the question; if she gave in, Nick and Tony would eventually find out, no matter how hard she tried to hide it.

Walker was a formidable opponent. He hadn't built a company like GeekBoy by being a soft touch in negotiations.

But she had an ace up her sleeve, too. What did he know about teens? He'd be too eager, press too hard, and Nick would back away himself. Her moody son didn't let anyone get too close.

She wouldn't bring it up, but if Walker asked

again, she'd tell him he could talk to Nick. Under her watchful eye. She wasn't about to leave them alone. Who knew what Walker would say to him?

She might have to give in to his demands, but she would do it her way. Her rules. Not Walker's.

RESTLESS AND UNUSED TO inactivity, Walker rode his bike down Main Street, headed for the mostly deserted county roads around Otter Tail. He'd have to go back to Chicago for a few days and take care of some business, but until then, he needed to burn off excess energy. Take out his frustrations on the pavement. He bent over the handlebars.

It had been stupid to kiss Jen. There were ten other ways he could have distracted her. Her taste had lingered in his mouth, and her touch feathered across his skin in his dreams.

The wind stung his cheeks like a slap in the face. Exactly what he needed to get his head on straight. He'd talked to one of Mary Haney's neighbors and found out she spent the winter in Florida. According to her friend, she usually came back to Otter Tail in May.

He couldn't wait that long. He'd asked his assistant in Chicago to find a phone number for her, and as soon as he had it, he'd give Mary a call and find out what she'd done with the contents of his father's house.

He was making progress. He'd have that picture soon.

As long as Mary hadn't thrown it away, like he'd ordered her to do.

Stupid to let his anger at his father cloud his judgment like that.

He was almost out of town when he spotted Nick and two other kids on Main Street. They stood in front of the same sports memorabilia store where he'd seen Jen and her younger son. Nick was talking, and the other two were listening intently.

He wouldn't have a better excuse to talk to the boy. Nick knew Walker had spotted him last night. It would be natural to ask him about it.

Squeezing his brakes, he rolled to a stop behind the trio. "Hey, Nick."

The boy looked over his shoulder and his eyes widened. "Uh, hi, Mr. Barnes." He said something under his breath to the boy and girl, and they took off. Were they the two he'd been with the night before?

"Do I look that scary?" Walker asked.

"Nah. They had to get home. I, uh, I do, too."

Walker leaned on the handlebars of his bike and watched Nick edge away from him. "What was going on last night?"

The kid rubbed his hands on his jeans and glanced down the street at his fleeing friends. "I was a little past my curfew," he muttered. "Thanks for not ratting me out, man."

"Are you going to tell your mom you were out until almost midnight?"

"Sure," he said warily.

"Think she'll be upset?"

"Nah. She doesn't care what I do."

The boy's left leg was bouncing, as if he was getting ready to bolt.

"Really? Didn't seem that way to me. She got pretty pissed at you for talking to me."

Nick shrugged. "The old stranger-danger thing, you know? She still thinks I'm a baby."

The kid was quick. "Is that right? Maybe I should ask her."

Nick licked his lips and looked around wildly. But his friends had disappeared.

"Unless you want to tell me what you were doing."

He scowled. "It's none of your business."

"You're right. It's not." Walker eased onto the leather seat of the bicycle and put one foot on a pedal. "See you later."

"Wait," Nick called as he pushed away from the curb.

Setting his feet on the ground, Walker looked over his shoulder and waited. Nick kicked at a rock on the sidewalk.

"All right," he muttered. He shuffled alongside Walker, who got off his bike to walk with him, his clips clicking on the sidewalk. After a minute, Nick asked, "When are you demo-ing *Sorceress* at the Harp?"

"Not sure yet," Walker answered. "I have to set that up with Quinn."

"Are you still, like, designing it?"

"Fine-tuning it."

"Yeah? I was hoping you'd, maybe, show me what you do."

"I could." They were walking past a gas station with a soft-drink machine by the door, and Walker said, "Want something to drink?"

"Cola. Please," he added.

Nick didn't say anything more until they reached a park along the Otter River. Skirting the playground, he headed toward a grassy spot on the riverbank. He took a long gulp of soda, and Walker set his bike on the grass and unscrewed the cap of his own sports drink.

The shouts of children on the playground drifted over, and an occasional fishing boat went by, heading toward Lake Michigan. The kid put the bottle on the ground between his feet. "It's Stevie," he said abruptly. "Me and Dave go over to her house on Friday and Saturday."

"Is Stevie the girl who was with you today?"

"Yeah."

"So why is it such a big secret?"

He blew out a long breath. "Mom won't let me go to Stevie's. And Stevie's parents would shit a brick if they knew we were there."

"How come?"

Nick glanced at him out of the corner of his eye. "You're not going to tell my mom, right? Because I'm telling you. That's what you said."

"I said it depended on what you were doing."

"That sucks, man."

"That's the deal. Take it or leave it."

He jumped to his feet and kicked a large rock into the water. Scowling, he said, "Stevie has to babysit her kid brother on Friday and Saturday night because her parents go out to party. But she's scared to be there by herself. So me and Dave go over after her brother's in bed."

"Can't she just tell her parents she's scared, and have them get another sitter?"

"God, no." He gave Walker a "you're so lame" look. "Her parents sell weed. They don't give a shit about Stevie. Once when her parents were gone, someone broke into the house and stole their stash. Stevie and her brother hid in the crawl space behind a bunch of boxes. Adam pissed all over himself."

Poor kids. "So now you stay with her while her parents are gone."

"Yeah. Me and Dave."

"Sounds like that could be dangerous."

Nick shrugged. "Stevie's not alone."

Walker stretched his legs out in front of him. "So why were the three of you running around last night?"

He blushed. "Her brother wasn't home. He was having a sleepover." He picked up another rock and heaved it toward the water. "Some kid who just moved to town. His parents don't know about the Meltons yet."

"And…?"

"And nothing. We were goofing off."

"You've done that before."

He lifted one shoulder. "Sometimes. We like being out when no one knows we're there."

"Are you peeping?" Walker asked sharply.

"Of course not!" Nick turned red. "That's gross."

"Then what are you doing?"

He crushed a twig beneath his shoe. "You know. Hiding from each other. Night games."

Night games? What was that? Walker hadn't run

through the town at night with his friends when he was Nick's age. But then, he hadn't done a lot of the things typical teens did.

"Are you drinking?"

Nick looked at him out of the corner of his eye. "Promise you won't tell my mom?"

"I can't do that, Nick."

The kid threw himself onto the ground. "We did once. Dave took some of his dad's beers. We all got sick."

Maybe it was normal for Nick to be goofing off with his friends. Trying beer. But what did Walker know about raising kids?

"You should tell your mom what's going on with Stevie. She'll help you figure out what to do."

"Don't you get it?" He jumped up again. "She told me to stay away from Stevie. But she's not the one selling weed." He threw his cola bottle toward a garbage can, and it bounced off. "She hates what her parents are doing." Nick shrugged one shoulder. "So I watch out for her."

Uh-oh. He recognized that gleam in Nick's eyes. He was sure he'd had the same expression on his face when he was that age.

About Nick's mother.

So much for trying to act like a parent. Walker had no experience handling this kind of problem.

But Nick was trying to do what he thought was right. Would most fifteen-year-olds take responsibility for protecting a friend? Walker had no idea, but he wanted to help. He liked him, this boy who might be his son.

"It's dangerous to be out after dark."

Nick snorted. "You sound like my mom."

"Think of another way to help your friend."

"This is the only way."

Nick was determined. Stubborn. Just like Walker at that age.

Was Nick his son? He turned and studied him, searching for the resemblance he'd seen earlier. Today the kid just looked like himself. As Walker watched him brood, he thought of all he'd missed.

If Nick was his, he'd missed his childhood. Half of his teens.

"You're giving me a weird look," Nick said.

"Just thinking about you and Stevie and Dave."

"Are you going to tell my mom?"

He should. It sounded as if Stevie and her brother weren't safe. "I'll think about it. I'll talk to you before I do anything, okay?"

Nick stared at him, his hands clenched into fists at his sides. "You're going to ruin everything," he said, then turned and ran out of the park.

Walker watched until he disappeared. What had

he expected? That Nick would welcome a stranger's interference in his life?

As far as the boy was concerned, Walker was just some guy butting in when it wasn't his business.

Maybe it *was* his business. It was time to find out.

CHAPTER NINE

THE DOOR TO THE STORAGE unit creaked as Walker rolled it up, and stale air drifted out. According to Mary, it hadn't been opened since she'd filled it, four years earlier.

"I couldn't throw all your mother's things away, dear," she'd said. "Not all those pictures and books that she loved so much." There had been a long pause. "I wouldn't want my memories tossed into the garbage."

Apparently, Walker had been paying rent on this cubicle ever since. His assistant had told him she'd done it without talking to him. That was why he paid her the big bucks, she'd said coolly. To make decisions he didn't want to be bothered with.

Boxes were stacked neatly in one corner, and the single lightbulb threw shadows on the concrete floor and the wall. The room was dusty and cold. A final resting place for bad memories.

All that was left of his family.

He pulled the top box to the floor and ripped open the duct tape holding it closed. It was full of books. Hardcover novels and biographies, mostly. He set that box aside.

The second box held more books. Paperbacks this time, and children's books. He drew them out and looked at them, one after another. *The Velveteen Rabbit. Charlotte's Web. The Polar Express.*

He remembered that one. His mother had cried every time she read the last line. He hadn't thought about the way his mother had read to him since long before she'd died in a car accident more than six years ago. She'd been on her way home from the airport in Green Bay after visiting him in Chicago. His father had blamed Walker for her death.

His hand wasn't quite steady as he replaced the books in the box.

He found the photos in the fifth box he opened. The framed ones had been wrapped in newspaper to protect them. The albums were cheap vinyl, cracked and faded. As if they'd been thumbed through many times.

One of the albums was white. The first page held three newborn-baby pictures—his mother's, his father's and his. A heart drawn in red marker enclosed all of them.

He turned the pages and saw pictures of him next

to his parents. The photo he remembered was on a page with a similar one of his father. They'd been taken at the same studio, and both babies were sitting on the floor.

His father wore a sailor suit and a matching cap. Walker wore a tiny dress shirt and pants—just as Nick had worn.

He'd been wrong; Nick's baby picture hadn't looked like Walker's. It looked like his father's. He touched the curve of the grinning mouth, the crinkled shape of the eyes. Maybe this would convince Jen he was right.

He gently took the two photos out of the album, then turned the page. There was a snapshot of all three of them. His father had one arm wrapped around his mother's shoulders, and the other held a laughing baby. Other images followed: his father taking him trick-or-treating on Halloween. Building with Lego blocks on Christmas morning. Helping him ride his first bicycle.

They were happy in those pictures. Smiling. How had this relaxed, proud father become the man who'd ridden Walker so hard? The man who had been angry enough to cut all ties because his son didn't want to be a fisherman? Bitter enough to refuse to speak to Walker at his mother's funeral?

He set the album aside and replaced all the other

photos in the carton. As he pushed the box back in place, he hesitated.

He shouldn't leave this stuff sitting in here. All these things had been important to his mother. Maybe his father, too.

He'd bring them back to Chicago with him. Maybe they would make his condo feel more like home.

"WHAT DO YOU MEAN, you don't have enough money? You just got paid."

The loud, surly male voice echoed over the background music in the drugstore, and Walker snapped to attention. That sounded like Nick.

Walker shoved a twenty dollar bill at the kid who worked in the photo section. "Here, keep the change."

He grabbed his envelope of prints and hurried to the front of the store. A blond woman stood in line, but he didn't need to see Nick standing beside her to know who it was. The shape of Jen's back, the color of her hair, the curve of her hip seemed to be implanted in his head.

He had a serious case of lust. For Jen Summers.

She said something to Nick, and although Walker couldn't hear her words, her sharp tone drifted back to him. Then Nick sneered at her and said loudly,

"You're not going to open it tomorrow. But I have a test tomorrow."

This wasn't the kid he'd talked to about Stevie the other day. That boy had been thoughtful. Kind. Willing to do anything to help his friend. This Nick was rude, sullen and disrespectful. Had Walker been that way with his own parents? Angry and insolent? Had he been that much of a pain in the ass?

Maybe that was the reason he'd fought with his father all through high school.

What did Nick want?

And what was Jen going to open? Walker edged forward, curious in spite of himself.

"Then you shouldn't have waited until ten minutes ago to tell me you lost your calculator," she was saying. "The school has a loaner program. You could have borrowed one."

"Those are for dorks and losers. No one else uses them."

"Then you've got a problem, pal. I can't give you the money."

"That's so unfair. You have the money."

"Yeah, I do. But it's already in my savings account."

"You could take it out if you wanted."

"Why should I?"

"Because someone stole my calculator."

"Really?" Jen asked. "Did you report it to Mr. Breen?"

"He couldn't do anything."

Walker noticed the kid didn't look at Jen.

"Translation—you lost it. So you pay for it."

She was at the counter now, and set down shampoo that had a picture of a lemon on the bottle, and a box of allergy medicine.

"You don't care, do you?" Nick raged. "I'm going to bomb that test, and you don't give a sh—"

"Nick." Jen glanced at the cashier and the people behind them in line. "You're making a scene," she said. "Stop it."

Before Walker realized it, he was behind them. "Are you guys all right? Need help with something?"

Jen spun around and her face reddened. Walker had no trouble reading her expression. He was the last person she wanted to witness their fight.

"We're fine, thanks," she said. She shoved her shampoo and medicine to the side and grabbed Nick's arm. "We were just leaving."

Walker followed them out the door. This was an opening, and he was going to take it.

"I couldn't help overhearing you," he said, following them down the sidewalk. "Nick needs a calculator?"

"Not your business, Walker."

Their kiss had been four days ago, and he hadn't seen her since. The Harp had been busy over the weekend, and she'd managed to slip out each night.

Now she was acting as if it they were nearly strangers, and that irritated him. He sure as hell hadn't been the only one affected by that kiss. He'd felt her response.

Time to remind her of that.

"It sounds as if you didn't bring enough money," he said, although that wasn't what she'd said. "Can I lend you what you need? Just until you get home?"

Jen took a deep breath. "It's not that I don't have the money. I need it for…never mind. Nick lost his graphing calculator and he doesn't have enough to pay for it."

She'd just handed Walker something he could use. "How about I lend it to him?"

"No, thank you. We're fine." She elbowed past him, pushing Nick ahead of her. The kid's shoulders were hunched, and Walker read embarrassment in every line of his body.

"It'll be a loan. He can work it off," Walker said.

"Work? For you?" Nick stopped and looked at him, his hope almost blinding. "Really?"

"Sure," Walker said easily. "I could use some

help with…" He thought quickly. "Getting ready to run *Sorceress* at the Harp."

"Awesome!" The kid was practically bouncing. "I could totally do that. That would be the cherry."

Jen pulled a ten-dollar bill out of her wallet. "Nick, go buy my shampoo and medicine while I talk to Mr. Barnes."

"But, Mom…"

"Nick. Go."

He opened his mouth to protest, shot a glance at Walker and shuffled back into the drugstore.

Jen turned to him. "I can't believe you said that. I told you to stay away from Nick."

"Are you going to do the DNA test?"

"No. I'm not changing my mind."

"Then this is a good way for me to get to know him. Without him suspecting anything." Walker gave her an easy smile. She wasn't the only one who knew how to turn the tables.

"What would 'getting to know him' accomplish? He's Tony's son. Besides, he doesn't need a new calculator. He can borrow one from the school."

"And become a loser? And a dork?"

Her mouth tightened. "You think this is funny? Those calculators cost almost a hundred dollars. This is a good lesson. He'll be more careful with his stuff."

"Maybe so, but this solves a lot of my problems. I need help setting up the game, programming to make it work on Quinn's system."

"I'm certain you're more than able to do the work yourself."

"Sure I am."

"You're backing me into a corner."

"I'm trying to. Test him or let him work for me. Your choice."

"What about those pictures you claimed you had? The ones that might look like Nick's baby pictures. Didn't that pan out for you?"

He held up the white bag. "Got them right here."

"Good. Let me see them, then you can get out of our lives."

She peered in the store window, then held out her hand. He slid the folder from the bag and passed her copies of the two photos.

She glanced at them, then gave them back. "You were a cute kid, but there's no resemblance."

She hadn't even realized she was seeing two different children—him and his father. "You barely looked at them."

"I didn't need to."

"I want to compare them side by side with Nick's," Walker insisted.

"Fine. Come over and I'll let you."

"How about today?"

"Good. Let's get this over with."

"I still want him to work for me." He would make her see the resemblance. "You can say the pictures don't look alike, but I still want him tested. And I want to get to know him. Or I'll get Tony's permission."

"You're a bastard."

"I am. So what'll it be, Jen?"

She peered in the store window, fuming. "I don't want him spending time with a bastard like you."

"I'll stop pressing you for the DNA test." For now, anyway. "I get programming help, and Nick earns some money."

"I'll pay for the damn calculator myself."

He couldn't resist pushing her. "Is it because of the other night?"

She held her ground. "What about the other night? What does walking me home from the Harp have to do with this?"

He struggled to keep the smile off his face. "Just wanted to make sure you weren't afraid of anything."

"You think I'm afraid of you, Walker?" She narrowed her eyes. "I know how to take care of my family. And myself."

"Glad to hear it. Nick wants to do this."

She looked in the window of the drugstore at Nick, standing at the counter, and her expression softened. "You're right. He's thrilled by the idea. You saw how excited he was. You made it so I can't say no."

"I'm using what I have."

"Fine. He can work for you until he pays off the calculator. But you do it at my house, where I can watch. I'll listen to everything you say to him."

"Okay, we'll work at your place."

Nick ambled out of the store and shoved the bag at his mother with a scowl. "Here's your stuff."

"Thank you," Jen said.

Walker reached for his wallet and handed Nick a hundred-dollar bill. "Go get your calculator and we'll figure out the details later."

Nick stared at him. "Really?" He looked at Jen. "You told him it was okay?"

"Get the calculator, Nick," she said.

"Thanks, Mom." He turned to Walker. "This is so awesome. Thank you, man." He rushed into the store.

The wind ruffled her hair, lifting the tiny tendrils that had escaped her ponytail. They glittered like gold in the sunlight. "Now that we've agreed about Nick, let's talk about you."

"We haven't agreed about anything. You forced

my hand." She shoved the strands of hair behind one ear.

"I didn't force your hand the other night. And if you feel the urge to kiss someone again…"

"I didn't kiss you. You groped me." She shifted her purse to the other shoulder. "You were trying to manipulate me. It didn't work. End of story. Forgotten as soon as I walked into the house."

Desire punched him like a fist as he watched her fingers tremble. "Really? You put it out of your mind?"

"Completely," she assured him. But she spoiled her airy dismissal by drawing a sharp breath when he held her gaze.

"Maybe you need a reminder."

"Don't think so," she said. "When something is important, I have a very good memory."

"Then I'll have to make this important."

The door of the drugstore banged open and she jumped. Nick came out, clutching a bag. "Thanks, Mr. Barnes. This was way tight of you. I needed it for a test tomorrow."

"Left it a little late, didn't you?" he said mildly.

Nick looked from him to his mother and his eyes narrowed. "You were talking about me."

"We were talking about remembering things." Walker glanced at Jen, who suddenly needed something in her purse. "Nick, why don't we go to the diner so we can talk about what I need you to do?"

"Cool." He stood straighter. "Is that okay, Mom?"

"You can talk at our house," she said. "Walker probably needs to see your computer."

"Is that okay, Mr. Barnes?" Nick asked.

"Sure." Walker smiled at him. "Whatever your mother says. I know we both want to make her happy."

"DARN IT," WALKER SAID lightly as they walked into her house. "I left my laptop in my car. Would you mind going back downtown and getting it for me, Nick? I'm parked outside the drugstore."

That was clever, Jen grudgingly conceded.

"That was *your* car? The Porsche?"

"That's it."

"Cool. Sure, I'll get it." He held out his hand for the keys.

"Me, too!" Tommy shouted. "I want to see the Porsche."

"Forget it, dork." Nick scowled. "What do you know about cars?"

"Porsches rock."

"Let him go with you," Jen said. She didn't want either of the boys around when she and Walker compared the pictures. Thank goodness both her parents were still at work.

"You're not touching anything," Nick said to his brother as they walked out the door.

As soon as it slammed, Jen went over to the bookcase and found the picture that was similar to the one Walker had shown her. It was at the back of the shelf, behind a collection of Nick's school photos.

She spun around. "How did you know I had a picture like that one of yours?"

"Last time I was here, I looked at your photos."

"You went through my things?"

"They were in plain sight and I was curious. Was I supposed to ignore them?"

She studied the baby smiling back at her. He'd been such a happy child, always laughing. She touched his mouth, then stuck out her hand. "Give me yours."

He set them side by side on the dining-room table. "This is me." He pointed to the first one. "This is my father." He touched the second.

"The pose is the same," she said, surprised.

"Same photography studio," he said, tapping the name embossed at the bottom of each photo. He put the picture of Nick beside his father's.

She moved it next to Walker's. Walker's face was

a little longer, her son's rounder. Nick's nose was bigger than Walker's. Walker's eyes were bigger than Nick's.

"They're not alike at all."

He put Nick's shot next to his father's. "How about this?"

Oh, my God. The two babies were almost identical. Same smile, same nose, same chin. She gripped the edge of the table and stared, her heart thundering.

"All babies at that age are unformed. Undefined. That's what you're seeing. Baby-ness." Her hands shaking, she switched the photos around again, putting Nick's next to Walker's. Like a barker at a carnival, trying to confuse the audience and muddy the issue, she realized with another spurt of panic.

"They could be twins."

"No. They couldn't." *But they could.*

"You're not seeing the similarity because you don't want to."

Oh, God, she saw it. And she'd think of an excuse in a minute. "You're seeing it because you *do.*" She gestured at the pictures. "They prove nothing."

"Nothing that would hold up in court. Unlike a blood test." He slid his photos back into the folder.

"Are you threatening me?"

"I don't want to do that…"

The "but" hung in the air.

"My answer is still no."

SHE'D STAYED IN THE kitchen, where she could hear Nick and Walker at the computer in the dining room. So far, she hadn't understood a thing they'd said. The two blond heads were close together, staring at the computer screen as they talked.

As she watched them, leaden fear settled in her stomach. Even from the back, they looked alike.

Because they were both blond. That was all. The baby pictures were a fluke.

Maybe they weren't.

She'd been studying Nick, trying to see any resemblance, since the first time Walker had spouted his wild assumptions. And she hadn't seen it.

The angles of their faces were different. Their eyes were a similar color, but not the same shape. Nick's hair was straight and Walker's was wavy.

He hadn't shown her any teenage pictures of his father. Would they look like Nick?

Maybe they would.

It couldn't be. She would have known, wouldn't she? How could a mother not know who her baby's father was?

That's why they have paternity tests.

If she was adamant about not testing Nick, Walker would probably give up. Especially if he got a dose of her son's sullen moodiness.

If Nick is Walker's son, he has a right to know.

It would do irreparable damage to his relationship with Tony. And with her. Walker wasn't interested in the hard work of parenting. He was trying to get back at her. That was all.

"Did you say you left your car on Main Street?" she asked Walker.

"Yeah," he said absently as he showed Nick something on the screen of his computer.

"You're going to have to move it. Or you'll get towed." She smiled to herself as she added potatoes to the roasting pan.

"Why?" He turned to her.

"That's what the signs say. No Parking During Rush Hour. And they take that seriously."

"Rush hour? In this Podunk town?"

She slid the roast into the oven. "We get a lot of traffic in the evening. People commuting between Door County and Green Bay."

"Fine."

As she cut zucchini and pea pods to stir-fry, she heard Walker say, "Start working on that code." The front door shut a moment later.

She stuck her head out of the kitchen and saw

Nick still glued to the computer. "He's coming back?"

"Yeah. We're right in the middle of something."

Damn it. "You're not done?"

"Duh, Mom. We're, like, working here."

"I want to see, too." Tommy, who'd come up from the basement, dropped into the chair Walker had abandoned.

"Get out of here, Tommy. You don't know anything about computers."

"Yes, I do. I have computer every Wednesday in school."

"Beat it, rat boy." Nick shoved his face close to his brother's. "This is my deal," he growled. "Go play with your baseball."

"Nope." Tommy settled into the chair as if he'd grown roots. "This is a lot more fun."

"Do I have to make you?" Nick said.

"You can try." His sneer was a mirror image of his older brother's.

"Tommy, Mr. Barnes was sitting there. You'll have to stand behind them if you want to watch." Jen took a breath, irritated that she'd have to break her rule about video games in the afternoon. She didn't want her other son to fall under Walker's spell. "Or you can play a video game downstairs."

"Really?" His eyes widened. "Cool." He scampered back down to the basement, and Jen sighed. Another thing to add to her Walker grievance list. She was going to have to start a second page.

CHAPTER TEN

"THIS IS DELICIOUS, Jen," Walker said an hour and a half later.

"Thank you." Jen sent a smoldering look at her mother, on the other side of the dining-room table, but she pretended not to notice. Her mom had invited Walker to stay for dinner, then arranged the places so he was sitting next to Jen. *Real subtle, Mom.*

He took another bite of meat and his arm accidentally brushed hers when he set his knife down. Just like he'd *accidentally* nudged her knee when he'd shifted in his chair. Jen pushed her plate away.

He touched her arm, sending prickles of heat over her skin. "Could I have the gravy, please?"

"Sure." She handed it to him. His knowing smile made her reach for a dinner roll. Instead of eating it, though, she slowly shredded it.

"Thanks for inviting me to dinner, Mrs. Horton," Walker said to her mother. "For including me."

If Jen hadn't known what he was doing, she'd think he sounded almost wistful. As if he'd never eaten a family meal before.

Was she supposed to feel sorry for him? The rich man who was trying to ruin her life and steal her son?

"I told you to call me Nell," her mom replied. She sounded delighted, and Jen closed her eyes. *Don't do it, Mom. For God's sake, no matchmaking.* "And you're more than welcome. We'll do this again soon."

No, we won't. "Nick, Tommy, would you clear, please?" Jen said, too loudly.

The boys pushed away from the table, and Walker stood, too. "Can I help?"

"Sit down, Barnes. That's the boys' job," Jen's father, Al, said. "Nick's been telling me how you're showing your game at the Harp. What's going on with that?"

Walker sat down again. He draped his arm casually over the back of Jen's chair, and the warmth from his skin made her neck hot. He stilled, as if he noticed her reaction, then began talking to her father. Jen shoved away from the table, forcing his arm off the chair, and grabbed the last of the plates.

Her father could entertain him for a while. She took a deep breath as she walked into the kitchen, but Walker's gaze burned into her back. Ignoring him, she scraped the dishes into the sink, then set them on the stained beige Formica counter.

"I'm going to make a sandwich for Walker. In case he gets hungry tonight," her mom said, grabbing a paper plate, some bread and the mustard.

"He's staying in a motel, Mom. What would he do with a sandwich?"

"What's wrong with you?" Her mother studied her with suddenly narrow eyes. "You haven't been very friendly tonight, Jen."

"Why did you invite him?" Jen whispered. "We're not friends."

"He was here. We were getting ready to eat. It would have been rude not to ask him to stay."

"Rude would have been fine."

Her mother glanced into the dining room, where Walker and her father were deep in conversation. "Too bad you didn't…" She clamped her mouth shut, but Jen knew what she'd started to say. *Too bad you didn't pick him instead of Tony.* Her mother had never liked her ex-husband.

"Don't you have to get ready for bowling?" Jen asked, trying to change the subject.

Her mom glanced at the clock. "Good heavens, yes." She giggled. "The time just flew during dinner."

Nell Horton didn't giggle. Jen stared at her, feeling queasy. "Mom—" she started to say, but her mother had bustled out of the room.

"Let's go, Al. We're going to be late for bowling." She smiled at Walker. "We bowl on Mondays, when Jen doesn't have to work. We're gone for several hours."

Horrified, Jen watched as her mother practically hauled her husband out of his chair and up the stairs. This had to be a nightmare.

Then Walker caught her eye and grinned. *Oh, God.* She turned away and wiped the counter down. Again. How fast could she get him out of the house?

She couldn't. Fifteen minutes later, her parents were gone and Walker was still in the living room, sitting on the couch, talking to the boys.

"Mom!" Tommy jumped up. "Do you know what Mr. Barnes used to do?"

"What?" she asked cautiously.

"He ran a fishing charter. He *fished* all day instead of working. How cool is that?"

"I'm sure he worked hard if he was on a fishing boat." She glanced at Walker and was surprised at the flash of anger she saw. "I don't think it was the same kind of fishing you do with your dad."

"Probably not," Walker said. Maybe she'd imagined the anger, because he smiled at Tommy. "We mostly took out big groups to catch salmon. Sometimes we caught fish to sell to Tomcat's."

"Yeah? I've eaten some of your fish! Grandpa buys chubs there all the time!"

"I stopped fishing a long time ago, Tommy. Probably before you were eating smoked chubs."

"How come? That's the coolest job in the world."

"Fishing is…fine…but I wanted to design computer games."

Nick was sprawled on the floor, typing on Walker's laptop, she noticed uneasily. As if it was the most natural thing in the world. "Fishing's okay," Nick said. "But I'd rather design games, too."

"Since you both like fishing, why don't we all go this weekend?" Walker suggested. "There won't be a lot of fish, probably, but you'll catch *some*."

Tommy dropped back onto the couch beside Walker. "On one of those big boats with all the fishing rods sticking up in the air? That would rock."

"Yeah, on one of those. I'm sure I still know some of the charter captains."

Walker was sliding right into her family. He'd already charmed both her boys.

She was still immune, thank goodness. "You're supposed to spend the weekend with your father," Jen reminded them.

"Dad texted me this afternoon," Nick said. "He can't make it this weekend. We're going next week."

Damn it.

"Sounds like we're set," Walker said. "Now, don't you guys have homework or something?"

After a prolonged goodbye, the two boys trudged down to the basement, where Jen had set up a small study area for them next to their bedroom. "Need help getting your computer together?" she asked Walker.

"Nope. I'm good."

"I don't want to keep you, then."

The silence stretched tight as she stood and stared down at him. He stared right back, slouching on the couch, making himself at home. To break the tension, she said, "Don't worry about the fishing trip. I don't expect you to take my sons out."

His eyes narrowed at the slight emphasis on the word *my.* "No problem. It sounds as though they like to fish. I'll enjoy showing them what I used to do."

"We'll talk about it later." If he was like Tony, he'd forget all about the promise.

"Fine." She picked up Tommy's baseball and mitt from the floor and put them on an end table. "I hope Nick was able to help you."

Walker raised his eyebrows. "You think a couple

of hours was worth a hundred bucks? No way. I may have enough money to cover the cost of the calculator, but you said this was about Nick learning a lesson. *Earning* the money to pay for his mistake."

"I'll give you the rest of the money, Walker." It would hurt, since she needed every penny, but it was better than having him around the house. Especially now that her mom was on one of her matchmaking kicks.

Could this nightmare get any worse?

"I won't take your money. The deal was Nick had to earn it. What time does he get off school tomorrow?"

"You can't come over tomorrow. I have to work."

"I won't say anything to him."

"My rules," she reminded him. "I have to be here."

"Okay. Then when can Nick and I get together next?"

"We'll figure it out. Some other time. I need to make sure they're doing their homework."

"Go ahead and check on them."

"You don't take hints very well, do you? I have things to do."

"Yeah, I got that." He held her gaze. "What kinds of things?"

She stood there for a long moment, trying to force him to go. He ignored her.

She gave in first and descended the stairs to check on the boys. They were actually working, apparently concentrating on their schoolwork. Giving her no excuse.

She headed upstairs slowly. But when she reached the living room, Walker was gone. Thank God. The door to the porch was open, although the light was off. He must have forgotten to shut it.

She began to swing it closed, when he said, "I'm out here."

She was tempted to lock the door. Squaring her shoulders, she stepped onto the porch.

It was cooler than the house, but not uncomfortable. Her mother had cleaned the porch for spring, and the room smelled of potting soil and the geraniums her mother had planted in the hanging basket near the window. For a moment, Jen didn't see Walker.

"Over here," he said, his voice soft in the semi-darkness.

He was sitting on the wicker love seat, hidden in the shadows. She could see his eyes and the darker shadow of his arms, draped across the back. He'd slouched down and stretched out his legs.

As if he wasn't going to leave for a while.

Her heart lurched, then began a hard, relentless pounding in her chest. What was she going to do with him? How would she get rid of him?

Except her treacherous hormones didn't really want him to leave.

"What do you want?" she asked.

He patted the cushion next to him. "Come sit down so we can talk."

Not in this lifetime. She grabbed one of the wicker chairs and dragged it close enough to see his face, then sat on the edge. "Go ahead."

His mouth twitched as he studied her. "I wanted to thank you for inviting me to dinner."

"That was my mother's idea. Next time she asks, tell her no."

"I had fun," he said. He sounded surprised. Bemused.

"It was dinner, Walker. Happens every night. It's not a big deal."

The wicker creaked as he shifted. "In my family, we usually ate in front of the television. I didn't know what was missing."

"Who helped you with your homework?"

"My parents both worked. When my father got home, he was too tired to do much with me." The wicker creaked again. "My mom, too, I guess."

"My parents worked, too. But they were never too tired to spend time with us."

"And now you do the same for your kids."

Was that wistfulness she heard in his voice? He

was rich and famous. He could buy whatever he wanted. "Our lives are hardly perfect."

"Especially not when some guy is trying to muscle in on your territory, right?"

"You think that's what this is? A turf war?" She moved her chair closer. "I'm trying to protect Nick. If he knew about this insane idea of yours, it would devastate him."

"I have to know," Walker said in a low voice.

"Why is this so important? Why would you even think it's possible?"

"We had sex. Nine months later, Nick was born. That's why I think it's possible."

"We used a condom."

"An ancient condom. I'd been carrying it around in my wallet for probably three years."

"That's a lot of wishful thinking."

"Hope springs eternal in the…uh, mind of a teenage boy."

"The odds are against it. It was one time, Walker. I was making love with Tony, too." The heat of shame burned through her, and she couldn't meet his gaze. "Lots more than once. I was in love with him. Of course Nick is his son."

"Love has nothing to do with making babies."

"In this case it did." She got up and stared out at the night through the high bushes in front of the windows. The streetlights were tiny cones of yellow behind the budding branches. "Tony and I didn't always use a condom."

"I thought you were one of the smart girls, Jen."

"I was." She stared blindly through the windows. "Love makes you do stupid things."

"Does it?" He stood and moved behind her. His breath tickled her ear and stirred the fine hairs on her nape. "What about lust?"

"Even worse." She wrapped her arms around her waist, remembering that day in the janitor's closet in high school. She'd never intended to have sex with Walker. She'd just wanted to persuade him to change Tony's grades. But her resolve had been weakened by their kisses. Completely destroyed when he'd touched her. "Lust changes everything."

"Mmm." He put his hand over hers, pressing it into her waist. "And it's so much fun."

His fingertips grazed her stomach, and she sucked in a breath. "What are you doing?"

"I remember how you taste." She felt his erection against her rear. "How you shiver when I do this." He nuzzled her neck and let his fingers trail down her hip. "Those tiny sounds you make when I trace your tattoo."

Need rose inside her like a hot wave. She was drowning in it, and he'd barely touched her. What would happen if she turned around and kissed him? If she slid her hands beneath his shirt to feel his skin.

If she let herself want him.

"No," she said.

His hands crept up her abdomen, and she put hers on top of them.

"You're only trying to make me change my mind."

"Believe me, Jen." He bit down lightly on the tendon in her neck, and she shuddered. "I haven't been able to stop thinking about the other night."

She couldn't tell him she hadn't forgotten, either. It would make her too vulnerable. "It was nothing, Walker." She tried to ease away from him.

"Let's test that theory." He lifted her hair from her nape, and her skin prickled where he'd touched her. He pressed a kiss below her ear, and she bit her lip.

His chest was hard against her back, and his heat surrounded her, even through the layers of clothing. The detergent he'd used to launder his shirt smelled like the air after a rain. The sweater he wore over it was as soft as a child's blanket.

His hands were still on her abdomen, and his thighs pressed into hers. He enveloped her in a cocoon of sensuality.

"Do you feel the chemistry?" he whispered into her ear.

God help her, she did.

He pulled slowly at her T-shirt, tugging it out of her jeans. "It was like this before." Cool air feathered across her abdomen. "Remember?"

"No." She drew in a breath when he slid his hand beneath the thin cotton and trailed one finger over her skin.

"Really?" He suckled her neck lightly as his fingers drifted higher. "Are you sure?"

"Ye-ess." She couldn't hold back the tiny sound that erupted from her throat when he brushed her nipple. She tried to turn, to face him, but his other arm tightened around her, holding her in place.

"What would I have to do to make you admit there's something between us?" He licked her earlobe, then grazed it with his teeth. "This?" He stroked her stomach, making her skin quiver. "This?" He pushed her bra up, then cupped one breast in his hand. His thumb circled, getting closer and closer. "Tell me, Jen."

She wanted to tell him to touch her. Admit that she wanted him. She bit her lip to keep from opening her mouth. To stop herself from begging.

"You're tough, Jen," he said into her hair. She thought she felt him smile. "But you're only tough on the outside. On the inside…" He touched her, finally, and her legs trembled. "You're soft. Tender. Delicious."

The hand holding her breast dropped down, and she heard the snap of her jeans opening, the rasp of the zipper lowering. "I know exactly where you're the softest."

He burrowed beneath her jeans, beneath her underwear, until he curled his hand around her, cupping her intimately. His other hand held her breast.

He kept her pressed against him. Possessing her. She moved in his arms, desperate for more, and had to swallow a cry when his fingers slid over her. "Tell me you want me."

"Walker..."

"Tell me, Jen."

His fingers glided over her again, and her hips moved in response. When he touched her nipple with his other hand, squeezed it gently between his fingers, she exploded. Her release swept through her, making her cry out.

He held her, kissing her neck as the tremors crested and receded and finally eased. Legs weak and trembling, arms shaking, she turned and put her arms around his neck.

He eased away from her and took a step back.

Aching, needing to hold him, she said, "What are you doing? What's wrong?"

"Nothing's wrong. Why? Didn't you enjoy it?"

"It was pretty one-sided, wasn't it?"

"Had to be." He zipped up her jeans. "No condoms. We don't want to make another baby."

He was so cool. So unruffled.

So detached.

"Why, Walker?"

"You wanted me." He stared at her for a long moment, then took another step back. "Good night, Jen."

The storm door clicked softly behind him. She watched until he was out of sight.

She sank onto the love seat, her legs still wobbly. It was a few minutes before the fog cleared. Before her breathing returned to normal, the heat in her body subsided. Finally, she took a deep, shaky breath.

He'd used her.

Just like she'd used him back in high school.

Not to get her to do something for him, but to make a point.

Was this how Walker had felt after that little session in high school? Used? Aching? Hollow inside?

She owed him for that.

But she wasn't going to sacrifice Nick to pay her penance.

CHAPTER ELEVEN

CHASED BY THE DEMONS he'd unleashed the night before, Walker cornered the bike too sharply. Why had he touched her?

Because he was a fool.

Wanting her, he'd only made himself more vulnerable.

A car honked at him, and he snapped his attention back to the road.

He rounded another corner and squeezed the brakes. His inattention had brought him to the place he'd been so carefully avoiding.

The high school.

Kids milled around the front door and mingled in the parking lot. Their day must have just ended.

As he passed the stadium, he heard the sound of kids shouting and cheering. He slowed when he saw the crowd gathered in a circle behind the scoreboard. Back in his day, it had been a popular place for fights. Apparently, the tradition was going strong, because two boys in the center of the group were a blur of motion.

The crowd shifted for a moment, and he saw a dark-haired boy swing wildly. The other kid's head snapped back when the fist connected with his face. Blood poured out of his nose.

It was Nick.

Before he realized what he was doing, Walker swerved to the side of the road and dropped his bike. The shouting and cheering faltered, then faded as he pushed through the teens. "Get lost," he snarled, and they melted away. Only Nick and the other boy remained, wrestling on the ground.

Walker grabbed both by the back of their shirts and yanked them apart. "Stop it!"

"Let me go!" The unknown kid twisted, and Walker released Nick so he could hold on with both hands.

"Not until you settle down." He held the boy's shirt until he finally stopped struggling. Walker looked at Nick, who was wiping his bleeding nose with his sleeve. "What's going on?"

"Nothing."

He let the other boy go. The kid glanced at Walker, and his eyes widened. His gaze darted furtively toward the stadium, then he took off running.

"Running away like a little girl, Boyd?" Nick

yelled after him, his voice thick with blood. "Chick-enshit!"

He swiped his hand across his face again, smearing another streak of blood on his sleeve. Walker pulled a wad of tissues out of his jersey, and Nick jammed them against his face.

"What were you fighting about?" Walker asked.

"Boyd's an asshole," he said, his voice muffled by the tissues.

Walker caught a glimpse of movement beneath the bleachers. Two more kids. "Do you two want to explain to me what was going on?"

Neither teen moved, then the smaller one strode out from the shadows. "It wasn't Nick's fault." It was a girl with short, choppy blond hair, a pointed little face and big brown eyes. "Boyd started it."

This had to be Stevie. "Stevie Melton?"

She lifted her chin. "Nick was...he was..." She bit down on her lip. "He was protecting me."

Nick moved the tissues away from his nose. "Boyd was shoving her, said he needed weed." He stepped closer to Stevie, but didn't touch her. "He ordered her to bring some tomorrow. I told him to get lost."

Dave finally emerged. "Boyd swung first. Dude had no choice. He had to fight."

What was Walker doing in this stew of teenage

testosterone? What did he know about handling kids this age? "Maybe you should have told a teacher about this."

Nick snorted. "Right."

Walker was being sucked into these teens' lives, and felt a moment of panic. He'd just wanted to find out if Nick was his son. That was all.

But back in high school, he would have done exactly the same thing if someone had been pushing Jen around. "So what are you going to do next time this happens?" And there would be a next time. With bullies, there always was.

Dave and Nick glanced at each other, and Dave smiled. "Dude, Boyd knew who he—" he jerked his head toward Walker "—was. A lot of the guys did. You're going to be, like, the most chilling guy in school. Boyd is gonna leave us alone."

Nick lifted one shoulder. "Whatever. I can take care of her."

"I can take care of myself, you dorks," Stevie said. She gave Dave a sharp elbow in the gut. "Way to back up your friend in a fight."

Dave clutched his stomach. "Nick told me to stay with you."

What was Walker supposed to do now? He wasn't responsible for these kids. But Stevie's prickly toughness and Nick's fiercely protective expression wouldn't let him walk away. "Figure out how to make sure this doesn't happen again."

"There's always another asshole."

"That's probably true," Walker said. "But you need a strategy."

He was good at strategies.

He should probably tell Nick that fighting never solved anything. That he, Stevie and Dave should have walked away. That's what a responsible par... *adult* would do. But Walker was proud of Nick. He'd done what he thought he should do, and likely considered the bloody nose a badge of honor.

Walker didn't think Jen would view it that way.

"Get cleaned up before your mother sees you."

The boy grimaced. "Mom and Tommy are probably at baseball practice by now. I can wash my shirt before she gets home." Nick looked around fruitlessly for a garbage can. He glanced at the No Littering sign, then wadded the tissues into a tight ball.

Walker hesitated, then held out his hand. He stuffed the mess into his pocket.

"Get some ice on your nose, too." Walker studied Stevie, who was chewing on her lip and bouncing on her toes. Like a small bird, she was poised to bolt.

Thank goodness Dave and Nick had been with her.

Walker was usually uncomfortable with his celebrity, but today he would use it shamelessly. "Is there a place where kids gather after school?"

"The Cherry Tree."

So that hadn't changed since Walker's high-school days. "Before we go home, let's stop in and get a soda. And some ice for Nick's nose. All of us. I'll tell you guys that I'll be giving out invitations to attend the first showing of *Sorceress*. And I'll make it clear that you three are in charge of the guest list." The booths were so close together he was bound to be overheard.

He could see the wheels turn in Nick's head. The kid smiled slowly. "That would be awesome, man."

BY THE TIME THEY slipped in the back door of Nick's house, the sweat from Walker's bike ride had long since dried and had begun to itch. The day had gotten colder, too, and he was anxious to take a shower. But he'd promised Nick he'd help him clean up.

The enticing aroma of roasting meat followed them down the stairs into the basement. "Your mom's cooking smells amazing."

"She's probably testing another recipe." Nick flicked on the light and headed for the washer and dryer against the wall. In one corner of the basement a small room had been framed out. The door was open and he saw two beds, with posters on the wall around them. On the other side, someone had laid a rug, strung some lights and made a desk out of a door and two bookcases. Two chairs sat in front of it, one at either end.

"Testing a recipe for what?"

"For her new restaurant. We're her guinea pigs."

Jen was opening a restaurant?

Nick stood at the sink, rinsing the blood out of his shirt.

"Your mom is going to find out about the fight, you know," Walker told him.

"Are you gonna tell her?"

Was he? That would be the responsible thing to do. The adult thing. Walker studied the dials on the washing machine. "When did these things get so complicated?"

"You don't know how to turn it on, do you?" Nick's voice was incredulous.

Walker shrugged. "How tough can it be?"

The teen opened a cabinet above the sink, pulled out a bottle and sprayed the remaining faint blood-stains on the shirt. Then he added detergent and turned the machine on. "Man, you design all those awesome games and you can't even do the laundry? What a loser!"

Nick shot him a look to see if he'd overstepped a line. Walker smothered a grin. "That's me. Laundry loser."

"My mom says you have to know how to take care of yourself." He grimaced. "She even makes me cook."

"Good for her," Walker said. "You want to eat, you should be able to cook."

"Hey, did you tell her about the deal with Stevie and Dave and me?" Nick asked, as if it was an afterthought. As if it didn't matter to him one way or another.

"Not yet." He doubted she'd want to listen to him. "I'm just trying to figure out the best way to bring it up."

"Maybe you could tell her about the fight, too, and calm her down. Explain why it had to happen."

Now Walker was supposed to be the go-between? Take Nick's case to his mother?

The way a father would?

Panic shot through him. *I wanted to know if he's my son. Am I going to act like a father?*

"I think it would be better if you told her."

"Hell, no." Nick looked at him out of the corner of his eye, judging his reaction to the swearing. "She doesn't understand guy stuff. And she likes you, so she wouldn't be mad at you."

She liked him? Right.

"And you like her."

You have no idea, kid. "I'll see how it goes when I tell her about Stevie and Dave, okay?"

"Better do it soon," Nick said, scowling. "I'll be in deep shit if she finds out from one of the other kids' parents."

"I'll try." This had been Walker's idea. He was the one who wanted to get to know Nick. He hadn't understood what that meant. The messiness. The complications.

So what was he going to do if Nick *was* his kid? Would he get involved in his life?

Nick would be family.

And what if he *wasn't* his father? Was he just going to walk away from Otter Tail and Nick?

And Jen?

WALKER RODE THE BIKE BACK to his motel slowly, trying to figure out how to make Jen listen to him, when all she probably wanted was to punch him. He hadn't figured anything out by the time he reached the small two-story building.

After wheeling the bike into his first-floor room, he began peeling off his clothes. As he dropped the jersey on the floor, he felt a lump in the pocket.

He pulled out the crumpled tissues Nick had used and tossed them into the wastebasket.

After a moment, he got them back out. There was a lot of blood on those tissues.

She would never agree to the DNA test now. She'd denied that the pictures were similar. She'd said he had no reason to think he was Nick's father.

She wouldn't see what was obvious even when it was right in front of her eyes.

She'd never know.

CHAPTER TWELVE

"THIS IS WAY COOL!" Tommy shouted, leaning over the edge of the boat as it bumped across the choppy waves. Walker grabbed the back of the boy's life jacket and hauled him back.

Jen should thank him, but she was afraid to open her mouth. Her stomach dipped with each rise and fall of the boat. She swallowed. She would *not* get sick. Why had she ever agreed to this?

Because she'd known that Nick and Tommy would have a great time. Nick was watching the bobbers carefully, waiting for one to disappear. His cheeks were flushed and his hair lifted in the wind. Tommy ran from one side of the boat to the other under Walker's close eye.

For someone who'd spent five years on a fishing boat, he didn't seem to like it very much. His mouth had been a grim line as they'd steered out of the protected area near shore and into the open lake. He'd set out twelve lines mechanically, his movements jerky, shoving the handles into the holders a little too hard.

They'd scarcely spoken since he'd arrived at her house at the ungodly hour of 5:00 a.m. They couldn't talk about what had happened the other night, not with the boys in the car. Jen was glad Nick and Tommy were with them.

"There's a school on the sonar," Charlotte Smith, the pilot, called. "We're right over it."

"Ease back a little," Walker said. The boat slowed, and Jen's stomach lurched again.

"One of the bobbers went under!" Nick yelled.

Walker plucked a rod out of its holster. "You're first. Reel it in."

Nick worked for ten minutes, winding the fishing line and drawing the rod back.

"Must be a big one. He's got a lot of fight." Walker grabbed a net and hung over the side. "I think it's close, though."

"Yeah." Nick grunted. After about a minute, he shouted, "Hey, I see it!"

In spite of her roiling stomach, Jen stood and saw a flash of silver in the water. Walker leaned over farther and scooped up the fish. He upturned the net on the deck, and the silvery fish flopped and twitched.

Walker picked up a short, stubby club and hit the fish sharply on the head.

Jen ran to the side of the boat and vomited until her stomach hurt. Walker handed her a towel and a bottle of water when she returned. "You okay?"

"Fine." She wiped her face, filled her mouth with water and spat over the side. "Sorry I got sick."

"Don't worry about it. We call it chum."

"That's disgusting."

He shrugged. "That's fishing."

Three hours later, they headed for the dock with four salmon in the cooler. Tommy had reeled in one, Nick another, and Walker brought in the final fish. Every time he landed one on the deck, Jen closed her eyes and put her hands over her ears.

He cleaned them at a table on the dock, then tossed the fillets into a cooler. They'd decided to smoke half of them, so drove to Tomcat's. Nick and Tommy went inside to figure out what smoked flavors they wanted, while she and Walker stayed in the car. The smell of fish hung heavily in the air.

"Thank you for taking them out," she said. "They had a great time."

"My pleasure."

"Really? You didn't look like you were enjoying yourself," she noted.

He stared at the building's weathered facade. "I hate fishing and everything that goes along with it.

I haven't eaten a fish since the last day I worked on my father's boat."

"If you hated it so much, why did you do it?"

"I didn't have a choice. I lost my scholarship to college. I needed a job. My father needed help on the boat. That's why."

She was the one who'd sentenced him to five years on a fishing charter. Five years of cold, rough water. Five years of clubbing fish to death. "I'm sorry," she whispered. "No wonder you hate me."

"I don't hate you, Jen." He looked at her then, his lips curving. "Couldn't you tell the other night?"

"That was sex," she said, her voice flat. "And power. It had nothing to do with hate or love."

He shifted in his seat. Somehow, he ended up closer to her. "I didn't plan that."

Heat rose up her neck.

If he was any other man...

Where were the boys? How long did it take to drop off some fish?

There was a long minute of uncomfortable silence before Nick and Tommy emerged from the tiny store. Walker asked them what they'd decided to do with their fish, and they debated Cajun versus lemon pepper flavors for smoked salmon the rest of the way home.

When they reached the house, the boys lugged

the cooler with the rest of the fillets inside. Instead of heading for his Porsche, parked at the curb, Walker waited for her. She tried to walk past him, but he put out a hand to stop her.

"How's your stomach?" he asked, pressing his hand over her abdomen.

Her muscles quivered under his palm. "It's fine." He dipped one finger beneath the waistband of her jeans as he moved away.

It was barely a touch. Just a quick sweep of a fingertip. Anyone watching would think it was merely an accident. But she sucked in a breath. "Thanks for the fish. We'll have them for dinner on Monday."

"You're not going to invite me?"

"Why would I? You said you hated fish."

"You're a good cook. I bet you could make fish palatable, even for me."

"Fine. Come on over."

She watched him as he sauntered to his car. She'd risen to the bait. You'd think by now she'd have learned to avoid the hook.

THE NEXT MORNING, the bell over the door to Frank's shop rang as Jen was measuring the space that would be her seating area. Frank was holding the other end of her tape measure, and he nodded toward the newcomer. "Be with you in a minute."

"No hurry."

Walker. The metal tab of the tape measure flew out of her hands and snapped Frank's knuckles as it rewound.

"Hey!" He shook his hand. "Take it easy."

"Sorry, Frank." She snatched the black metal case from him. "I'll look at the back room while you take care of your customer."

She hurried through the door into Frank's office. His desk was a mess, the piles held in place by boxes of sports cards. A frame holding a signed Brett Favre jersey leaned against the wall next to a filing cabinet. A milk crate held autographed baseballs. Beyond the desk were mostly empty metal shelves.

She could put a kitchen in this space. She tried to visualize where everything would go, but Walker's voice in the background distracted her, and her body responded.

What was he doing here? She doubted he collected baseball cards.

The talking stopped, but the bell over the door didn't ring. Was Walker waiting for her? He clearly didn't know the meaning of "no." Or "get lost."

When she returned to the front of the store, he was just slipping a small brown bag in his pocket.

"Hello, Walker," she said, wondering what he'd bought. "I had no idea you were a sports fan."

"Huge one," he answered. "Cubs season tickets."

"Bunch of losers."

"This is the year."

"It always is, isn't it?"

"Cubs are great," Frank said. "We sell a lot of Cubs stuff."

She turned to the shop owner. "I think I have everything I need for now. If you'll get those utility bills together, I'll stop in and pick them up."

"Sure. I'll dig out a lease, too."

"Great. Talk to you soon."

She walked out the door, intensely aware of Walker behind her.

"You're renting this place?" he asked. "What for?"

"I don't think that's any of your business."

"Just curious."

He kept pace with her as she headed down the block, and finally she sighed. "I'm opening a restaurant there."

"I thought you had a catering business. Like at Quinn's wedding."

"I'm only doing that to scrape together enough money for the restaurant. I didn't intend to do it so soon, but…"

"But I showed up in Otter Tail, and you want to get away from the Harp."

"Not everything is about you, Walker."

"Now you've hurt my feelings." He slipped an arm through hers. "You're going to have to kiss them and make them better."

"Stop it." She broke away. "What do you want?"

"Why that spot?"

"Because it's available. It's on Main Street. Tourists driving through to get to other Door County towns will pass it. Some of them will stop." She walked a little faster. "I have to head home and get ready for work."

"You don't have to be at the Harp for three hours. We need to talk about Nick."

"The answer is still no. We're not doing the test." She glanced at him out of the corner of her eye. "And if you want him to keep working for you, you better not bring it up again."

"When did you become such a ball buster?"

"You have no idea how tough I am." She'd learned her lessons well while she'd been married to Tony. Show no weakness. Give away nothing that could be exploited. Don't back down.

"Okay, tough girl. Did you know Nick goes out at night?"

"What?" She stared at him, not sure she heard him correctly. "He does not."

"And you know this because you're keeping an eye on him?"

She sucked in a breath. He'd managed to distill all her guilt into one sentence. "Go to hell, Walker."

CHAPTER THIRTEEN

SHE ONLY WANTED TO GET home. To be safe.

Away from him.

"Jen. I'm sorry." When she tried to step around him, he moved with her. "That was a cheap shot. It was unfair and untrue."

"I *am* gone almost every night."

"But you're there during the day. Please. I promised him I'd talk to you about this."

She whirled to face him, furious. "When have you talked to him by yourself?"

She let him steer her to the park, where they both sat on one of the benches. The play area was deserted. A blue-winged teal flew over and landed on the river with a tiny, faraway splash.

"I saw him running through an alley the night I walked you home. Late. With a couple of other kids." Walker rested his elbows on his knees and stared down at the grass.

That was the night he'd kissed her. "Why didn't

you speak up as soon as you saw him? So I could deal with it immediately."

He shifted on the bench as if he was uncomfortable. "I was pissed off about Nick. I guess I was trying to get even with you." He slanted her a look. "Know something about him you didn't know."

She leaped off the bench. She couldn't bear to be that close to him. "He's not a pawn in your game. He's a child. What he was doing was dangerous. You should have told me."

"You're right. I should have. That's why I'm telling you now." His gaze shifted to a boat on the river.

"What else?"

He shoved his hand through his hair. "I'm sorry, okay? It was stupid. I wasn't thinking about what was best for Nick."

"You were playing a stupid power game. At the expense of my son."

Maybe his son, too.

"He was with two other kids. Stevie Melton and a guy named Dave. I forced him to explain what he was doing. I used the threat of ratting him out to you."

She sank back down on the bench. This wasn't good. Nick would normally put up every barrier in his arsenal at a threat like that. Did her son feel some connection with Walker? Blood calling to blood?

That was ridiculous. Fanciful.

She didn't do fanciful.

He smiled, a tiny curve of his lips. "He said you'd listen to me, because you liked me."

"Shows what he knows," she muttered.

"Here's the deal. He and Dave go over to the Meltons' house on Friday and Saturday nights."

"What?" She swung around to face him. "He knows he's supposed to stay away from that family."

"He's doing a good thing, Jen." Walker told her about Stevie's parents and the drugs and the intruder, about Nick and Dave trying to protect the Melton kids.

"I had no idea. Those poor children."

Sunlight filtered through the trees, making lacy designs on the grass, and the air was warm. But goose bumps rose on her skin as she thought about the danger the kids were in. And now Nick, as well.

"Nick likes Stevie. I've known that for a while, but the Meltons have always been bad news. They were a few years ahead of us in school—in my sister Pam's class—and they were troublemakers even then." Jen shook her head, remembering Stevie's pinched face and tense shoulders. "I'm ashamed I never tried to help Stevie or Adam. Something has to be done."

"I agree." Walker put one arm across the back of the bench. He wasn't touching her, but she slid farther away.

"There was a fight a few days ago," he continued. "Some kid named Boyd was hassling Stevie for marijuana, and Nick stood up for her."

Jen couldn't repress the flash of jealousy. "Nick told you about it?"

"No. I was riding my bike past the school when it happened. I pulled them apart."

"Nelson Boyd is a spoiled brat." She remembered his bullying and tantrums at birthday parties when the kids were much smaller. "I'm not surprised he's progressed to pushing girls around. He'll end up like the Meltons."

"What are you going to do?"

Surprised, she glanced at him. Tony would have told *her* what to do. Given her what *he* thought was the solution.

"I'll start with Nick," she said slowly. "He should have some ideas how to help Stevie and her brother. Ultimately, though, I'll have to call child services. Stevie and Adam are probably going to be taken out of the home. Rusty and Lauralee Melton will be angry, and it will get ugly."

"Do you have room in your house to take them in, at least temporarily?"

"We could make room, but we've got to come up with a long-term solution. If he's being so protective of Stevie, the two of them living in the same house isn't a good idea."

"I didn't think of that, but you're right. I saw the way he looked at her."

"My baby is growing up," she said. An image of Nick as a newborn filled her mind. Helpless, completely dependent on her. He wasn't a baby anymore, but she still wanted to protect him.

"He's fifteen. Not a child."

"I know. It's just…" She looked at the river as a shimmer of light reflected off the water. That was the reason tears pricked her eyes. It had nothing to do with another geeky boy, sixteen years earlier. A boy on whom *she'd* inflicted pain. "Nick's always seemed to be more interested in games and his buddies than, you know, girls."

"Even geek boys like girls," Walker said drily.

She'd have to have another talk with Nick. She wished she could leave it to Tony, but he'd turn it into a joke. That was his fallback when something made him uncomfortable. Nick would be self-conscious and he'd tune his father out.

Tony meant well, but he never thought about how to handle the boys. Never thought about the message he was sending when he didn't take things seriously.

It was impossible not to compare Tony to Walker. It wasn't fair to Tony. He did the best he could. But Walker was the one Nick had confided in.

Nick would never have gone to Tony for help.

It was a sad situation, both for the boys and for herself. She and Tony had been in love once. So eager to start their life together. But everything had started to unravel after he had to go directly to the minor leagues.

Because he'd lost his baseball scholarship.

Because she'd seduced Walker into changing Tony's grade.

Because they'd all been caught.

"Hey." Walker jostled her arm. "Where did you go?"

She stared at the sunlight bouncing off the river. She didn't want to go back there, didn't want to face the careless, cruel girl she'd been.

Maybe she should tell him about the gradual dismantling of her marriage, the way it had hollowed out until nothing was left but a shell of bitterness and anger. Maybe it would make him feel better about his five years on that fishing boat.

Did she want to open herself up to Walker? Make herself that vulnerable?

"Jen? What are you thinking about?"

"Nothing that has to do with Nick. Nothing that's any of your business."

WALKER WATCHED JEN AS SHE stood in front of him, the sunlight turning her hair to gold.

She'd fight him to the death over Nick. A part of him admired her stubbornness. She would do whatever she thought necessary to protect her son.

She turned to face him. "What do you want from me, Walker?"

To get you naked.

His mouth curved as he imagined what she'd do if he said that. At least she didn't have a baseball bat handy. "For starters, I don't want to be your enemy."

"You want my son," she said, her voice flat. "That puts us on opposite sides."

"Does it have to be one or the other? Can't he be our son?"

"He already has a father."

"Is there any reason he can't have two fathers?"

She scrubbed her hand over her face and dropped onto the bench. "How am I supposed to tell Nick that I slept with you while I was dating Tony? What would he think of me if he knew that?"

"There are no easy answers, Jen, but we can figure them out together."

"Together? I don't want you in our lives, Walker. Don't you get it?"

"Give me your hand," he said.

She stared at him for a moment, then slowly complied. Her fingers were chilly in his and a little chapped. She worked hard—for her kids. For her dreams. Another thing he liked about Jen.

He pressed her palm against his chest, let her feel his heart racing. As she stared at him, her eyes darkened. Her breathing became more shallow.

He lifted her hand and pressed a kiss to it. She stared at him for a moment, her lips parting, then she pulled away.

"You're telling me you want me? The woman who took away your college education and sentenced you to five years on a fishing boat? Kind of hard to believe, since you can have any woman you want."

"Maybe the right one hasn't come along yet."

"Right. The dateless-geek card won't work with me, Walker," she said. "I read *People* magazine. Who was that last actress you had on your arm? The one who was nominated for an Oscar?"

"Okay," he conceded with a smile. "I'm not lacking for dates. But Missy Singer isn't exactly real."

"Parts of her certainly aren't," she said.

He laughed. "And you wonder why I want to spend time with you?" Jen in her jeans—worn white at the stress points and thin in the knee—and her soft, faded sweater, was as real as it got. And more enticing than any of the so-called beautiful people he'd dated.

Lately, he'd become a big fan of real.

She glanced at her watch. "I have to get ready for work."

"I'll walk you home."

"Not necessary." Her barriers were up again.

"Of course it's not. I want to." In the sunlight, the buds on the trees were a brilliant green. The first daffodils were opening and the tulips weren't far behind.

"Is that pizza place in Sturgeon Falls still open? The one with the best pizza in the county?"

"Danilo's? Yeah, it's still there." She glanced at him suspiciously.

"Great. You're off Monday, aren't you?"

She shook her head. "No, Walker. I'm not going to Danilo's with you."

They didn't speak as they left the park and waited for a car to pass.

What was going to happen when he got the results of that DNA test back? If it was positive, would Jen forgive him?

CHAPTER FOURTEEN

"IS THIS PART OF YOUR master plan, Walker?" Jen had to raise her voice to be heard over the Go Karts roaring around the track in front of her.

"What master plan would that be?"

"The 'innocent and bewildered' look isn't a good one for you. You're charming my sons. Giving them the evening of their dreams. You have an ulterior motive." He couldn't possibly want her that badly. Although the thought made her shiver, it was a little hard to believe. This was a guy who'd dated Missy Singer, after all. Why would he want the woman who'd used him—slept with him—while she loved someone else.

"Of course I do." He nudged her hip with his. "I'm trying to charm their mother into going out with me next Monday."

Was this part of an elaborate revenge scheme? It had to be.

She couldn't let him charm her into forgetting that.

She'd watched Nick and Walker over their pepperoni pizza. *Was* Nick his son? What would she do if he was?

The smell of diesel fuel drifted past them in a blue cloud of smoke. The Go Karts were on the other side of the track now, and the noise wasn't as loud. "I hope they're having a good time," he said, watching them. "It sounded like fun."

"You want to be out there, too, don't you?"

"Doesn't it look like fun? Don't you want to try it?"

"I'd worry about being overcome by the testosterone fumes."

"It's a well-known hazard of Go Kart racing." He nodded gravely. "Hundreds are affected every year." He grabbed her hand. "Let's try it."

"Didn't you ever drive one of those things when you were a kid?"

"No." The laughter disappeared from his face. "Come on, I'll race you."

FIFTEEN MINUTES LATER, laughing, she staggered off the track with Walker, Nick and Tommy. Her legs were still vibrating and her ears ringing.

"You were awesome, Mom," Tommy said. "You beat all of us."

"She cheated," Walker said. "Otherwise, I would have won."

"No way, man," Nick said. He was actually smiling. "How do you cheat at Go Karts? You came in last. Loser."

"What's next?" Walker asked. "You guys want to play miniature golf or video games?"

"Games!" Tommy yelled.

"Yeah, me, too," Nick said.

Walker shoved a twenty into the change machine, then handed Nick the tokens that gushed out. "Here you go. Your mom and I are going to play miniature golf."

"Nick, keep an eye on Tommy," she couldn't stop herself from saying. "And neither of you leave the arcade."

"Yeah, yeah," Nick said, scanning the machines for his favorite. "See ya."

As Walker led her outside into the cool spring air, she glanced over her shoulder. Both boys were standing in front of game consoles, ignoring them completely.

There were very few people at the amusement center—on a Monday night in April, there weren't many tourists in Door County. The miniature-golf area was deserted. A bored teen handed them putters, and they stepped onto the empty course.

"You recovered yet?" Walker asked.

"I may eventually get my hearing back," she

said. "And my rear end probably won't be numb for much longer."

"Want me to massage it for you?" He slid his arm around her waist and let his hand drift toward her hip. She batted it away.

"These are the only games I'm playing tonight."

He grinned and grabbed a couple of balls from the bin. "You want orange or green?"

"What are you doing, Walker?" she asked quietly.

He turned to face her, then dropped the golf balls back into the bin. "Having fun. I hope you and Nick and Tommy are, too."

"Of course we are." She nodded at the Go Kart track. "What's not to like? Go Kart racing? An almost unlimited supply of tokens for the video arcade? They're in heaven."

"What about you?"

"I love watching my sons having fun. Being happy. Not arguing. I'm in heaven, too," she said lightly.

"But…?"

She set the golf club against the rail and stared at him, waiting.

"Sometimes a game is just a game." He looked at the giant blue-and-red Aladdin's head over one hole, the faded wooden water wheel over the next, and she saw wistfulness in his expression. Longing. "It caught my eye as we drove past. It looked like the kind of place high-school kids would hang out."

And he'd never done this as a teen. "You didn't have a lot of fun in high school, did you?"

He swung the golf club back and forth. "No. I thought there was one time when I did. But I was mistaken."

She should be used to it by now—the body slam of guilt. Regret. "As much as I'd like to, I can't change the past." She shoved her golf club back in the bin. "This was a mistake."

"I'm not asking you to change the past. The future? Maybe."

"They can't be untangled," she said wearily. "What happened back then affects everything."

"Does it?" He touched her cheek and let his hand drift to her neck.

Her mouth went dry. Stupid to be stirred up when it was part of his game. His revenge. She started to push him away, but his hand slid around to her nape and he pulled her closer. He drew them to the shadows next to the Eiffel Tower standing over the third hole.

"I think you made a wrong turn," she managed to say.

"The guys in gym class used to talk about

making out here." Their bodies were almost touching. His hands drifted over her back and tucked her against him, and a lovely heat swirled inside her. "No one can see us."

"I knew you had a plan."

"What could be more romantic than making out at the Eiffel Tower?" He bent and kissed a spot just below her ear that made her shiver. "I want you." He moved his mouth lower, and she trembled. "I think you want me. It's not complicated."

It was complicated as hell. They weren't two people who'd just met and were having a vacation fling. Even without the issue of Nick, there was too much history between them. Too much betrayal. Too much pain.

How could he ignore that? How could she?

"A kiss won't hurt," he whispered in her ear. Then he gently suckled her earlobe, and she shuddered. Desire rose like a tide inside her, swamping everything—her reason, her will, her self-preservation. She wanted nothing but his hands on her. And hers on him.

She turned her head to find his mouth, and wound her arms around his neck. As he kissed her, he drew her deeper into the shadows, turning her so that she was almost completely hidden beneath the low branches of a maple tree. One of the paddle-shaped seeds fluttered down and skimmed over her face, and he brushed it away.

His fingers trailed down her cheek and onto her neck, and he followed it with his mouth. He unzipped her sweater and pushed it to the side, then nibbled on her collarbone. He'd barely touched her, but she was burning up.

Yanking his shirt from the waistband of his jeans, she smoothed her hands over his abdomen, lingering when his muscles jumped beneath her fingers. His skin was hot, and he trembled when she stroked the coarse hair on his chest.

"You're making me crazy, Jen," he groaned. "I want to rip your clothes off and make love to you right here." He backed her up until her legs bumped against the wooden rail of the fence, and fumbled with the snap of her jeans.

The last time he'd done that it hadn't been about desire or even lust. It had been about power and control. The memory was like a splash of cold water, and she found the strength to step away from him.

"That's a lot more than a kiss."

He reached for her again. "I didn't say where I was going to kiss you."

His fingers slid into her waistband, and the backs of his knuckles brushed against the sensitive skin of her lower abdomen. Need, dark and potent, overwhelmed her reason.

With a supreme effort, she moved out of his reach. "You're way too fast for me, Walker." She'd slept with only two men in her life—never in such a public place—and sex with Tony had been practically nonexistent in the last two years of their marriage. That was the only reason she was reacting so strongly to Walker. "Let's get the boys and go home. This is a school night."

His face was in shadow, but his gaze burned through her.

"Yeah. You're right. This isn't the time or place." He trailed one knuckle down her cheek, then took her hand, leading her into the lights. "Just like last time."

His hand was shaking in hers.

"Although," he said, "that didn't seem to stand in your way back then."

AS THEY DROVE THROUGH the darkness, the boys chattered about the video games they'd played. Walker knew every one of them, and he, Nick and Tommy exchanged strategies for winning. They sounded like a family after an evening out, she thought uneasily.

Except Jen knew better. Was that what he was

trying to do? Show her how they could've been a family? If she hadn't manipulated him, used him then forgotten about him.

"How did you and Mom do at miniature golf?" Tommy asked, interrupting her thoughts.

"Not so great," Walker replied. "I don't think that's my game."

"Miniature golf is stupid," Nick said.

"I think I agree with you," Walker said, looking straight at her.

Before she could say anything, he glanced over his shoulder. "Hey, Nick, I need to fine-tune more of the programming for *Sorceress* tomorrow. Will you have time after school?"

"Yeah! That's great! I mean, sure. I can work tomorrow."

"Good. Three-thirty at your house okay?"

"That's okay, right, Mom?"

"Of course." She managed to keep her voice light. Impersonal.

Walker Barnes was even more dangerous than she'd thought.

CHAPTER FIFTEEN

THE PUB PATRONS APPLAUDED as the band finished "Suite: Judy Blue Eyes" with a drum flourish. When Paul and Hank stood and set their guitars down, Walker felt a hum of anticipation. Shortly after the band took their break, Jen usually emerged from the kitchen, finished for the night.

It had been a long time since he'd taken the time to seduce a woman. A long time since he'd needed to. Jen certainly wasn't awed by his money. He smiled to himself. Far from it. She'd insisted on paying her share of the pizza the other night.

"You look pleased with yourself."

It was the drummer from the band. Walker straightened. She was a friend of Jen's. He'd seen the two women talking.

"I'm Delaney." She slid onto the stool next to him.

"Yes, I remember you from the receiving line at Quinn's wedding. Walker Barnes. Any reason I shouldn't be happy?"

Quinn set a tall glass of something clear in front of her, and Delaney smiled in thanks. She took a drink, then wiped a trickle of sweat from her temple. Her short blond hair was plastered against her forehead, and the T-shirt she wore had dark sweat stains on it.

She leaned one elbow on the bar as she studied him. "Depends. What are you up to with Jen?"

"Are you always this suspicious?"

"Yep." Her straw made a sucking sound as she drained the glass.

"I'm holding my breath, waiting for her to walk out that door and dazzle me. I can barely contain my excitement." He finished his Leinie and set the glass down.

She frowned. "You mess with her and you mess with all of us," she said. "I want to make sure you know that."

"Got it. Hurt Jen and the skinny drummer will beat me up."

"You've got that right, pal," she said. "Just wanted to be clear."

"Clear as your drink," he assured her.

Would any of his friends protect him like that? Stand in front of anyone who might hurt him?

Kirit, maybe. They'd been tight for a long time, although their relationship was mostly business now. Walker couldn't think of anyone else.

He suspected that everyone in the pub would jump to Jen's defense.

"You looking out for her, too?" Walker nodded at a blonde who was talking to one of the guitarists, who looked agitated. "Maybe you ought to go talk to your buddy in the band."

Delaney glanced at the couple, then rolled her eyes. "Paul and Laura are a couple of dumb-asses who have to work things out themselves. They're on their own."

"At least I'm not a dumb-ass," Walker said lightly.

Delaney narrowed her gaze as she pushed off the stool. "I hope not, Barnes."

As he watched her ease her way through the crowd, Quinn appeared on the other side of the bar. "You waiting for Jen?"

"Why? Are you going to warn me off, too?"

"What are you talking about?"

Walker nodded at Delaney, who was chatting with Maddie. "She threatened to kick my ass."

Quinn laughed. "That's our Delaney. The adrenaline gets going when she's playing. She needs an outlet."

He was an outlet? Walker smiled reluctantly.

The lights went off in the kitchen. Taking out his wallet, he threw several bills on the bar and stood. "That's my cue. Talk to you later, Quinn."

Jen emerged through the swinging door, and stopped at the edge of the crowd. Her ponytail was a little ragged, with wisps of hair curling around her face. Her T-shirt was wrinkled from her apron, and her jeans sat low on her hips.

She scanned the pub and stilled when she saw him watching. Their eyes met.

JEN WATCHED WALKER heading toward her. She'd tried not to look for him. Promised herself she wouldn't. But she had, and now she needed to get out of here. How could she be looking forward to seeing him? Anticipating more of those devastating kisses? He was a reminder of all the hateful, ugly parts of herself she'd tried to leave behind.

Blindly, Jen shoved her way out of the pub, her heart racing, her chest tight. She leaned against the rough wooden siding and sucked in a deep breath of the cold, clean air and tried to calm herself. She wasn't that person anymore. She'd changed.

But she couldn't focus on that when Walker was around. He was a reminder of everything she wanted to forget about herself.

She began walking toward her parents' house.

The pub door opened and footsteps echoed behind her. She knew who it was.

"Go away."

"Why should I?" Walker said. She could hear him coming closer.

"I don't want you to walk me home."

"Why not?"

"Because you remind me of the worst part of my life." Her voice was barely above a whisper, carried away by the wind.

"Bad memories can be replaced," he said. *He'd heard her.* "Let's make new ones."

"Don't you get it? We can never get beyond the past. What I did to you." She walked faster, but he kept up with her easily. "Why would you even want to?"

"Give me a little credit, Jen. I know people change. We're not stuck with the teenage version of ourselves."

The door of the Harp opened again, then closed with a thump. Walker glanced over her shoulder and steered her away from the bar.

"People do change." She hoped she had. "But sometimes, the past can't be left behind."

As they walked down the deserted street toward her house, the footsteps behind them sounded louder. As if the people were catching up. The sidewalk was lined with shops, but everything was closed. His arm tightened, and he abruptly shoved her around a corner.

He stood in front of her and tensed as footsteps neared the corner. The two figures, still in deep shadows, stopped abruptly when they saw him.

"Did you want something?" Walker asked in a neutral voice.

"We want to talk to her," the man said.

Jen stepped out of the doorway. "Rusty? Lauralee? What's going on?"

Rusty Melton was shorter than Walker, but bulging with muscles. His shaved head gleamed in the streetlight, and dark tattoos ran down both arms. Lauralee was even shorter and wore a tight skirt and a low-cut blouse.

Rusty stared at Jen, flexing his fists, clearly enraged. She tensed, ready to run. Walker stepped in front of her again.

"Out of my way, pretty boy," Rusty said. "Our business is with her."

"These are the Meltons," Jen told Walker. "Stevie's parents."

Rusty flexed his fist, and Lauralee crossed her arms over her chest.

"Why did you follow us, Rusty?"

"You sent the cops to our house," he said, and Walker tensed beside her. Rusty spat on the sidewalk. "I've seen that boy of yours sniffing around Stevie."

"You're putting your children in danger. You should be ashamed of yourself," she told him.

"That's none of your business."

"Someone has to care about them."

Walker put his hand on her shoulder, and she could feel him struggling to control himself.

"You think I don't care about my kids?"

"Sure doesn't look like it, Rusty." She glanced at the woman. "What are you thinking, Lauralee?"

"I do right by my kids," the woman said. "Nobody can say otherwise."

"I'm saying otherwise."

Rusty lunged for her, and Walker stepped in front of her, saying, "You have to go through me first."

"I'm calling the police, Walker," Jen said.

She tried to pull Walker back, but he shook her off. "Good idea." He watched Rusty steadily.

"You think you can take me?" The burly man raised what looked like a switchblade and extended it toward Walker, but before he could release the blade, Walker kicked it out of his hand. It flew into the street and skidded halfway across. With shaking fingers, Jen punched in 911.

"What the hell?" Rusty started for the knife, then swung around to face Walker, his eyes bright with rage. He cocked his arm back and let his fist fly.

Walker dodged him easily and kicked him in the

gut. The man bent over with a grunt, and Walker chopped his hand against the side of Rusty's neck. The drug dealer collapsed on the sidewalk, unmoving.

"You killed him," Lauralee shrieked, leaping at Walker, her fingers curled into claws. She gouged his face before he managed to grab her arms, then hold them tightly as she thrashed.

"Stop it," Walker said, shaking her. "Settle down."

By the time the cops arrived, Rusty was on his hands and knees, retching in the gutter. The officers handcuffed a screaming, cursing Lauralee and put her into one of the squad cars. As they yanked her husband to his feet and handcuffed him, Walker and Jen explained what had happened.

Jen pulled a tissue from the pack in her purse and pressed it to the scratch on Walker's face. He told Brady Miller about the knife and kicking it into the street. Lauralee alternately cried and swore, while Rusty hurled threats at both of them.

"Your kids home alone, Melton?" Brady said to Rusty. When he answered with a curse, Brady looked at Jen and Walker. "We'll call county Child Protective Services."

"Tell them the kids can stay at my parents' for tonight," Jen said.

She waited until Pete Meyer put Rusty into the other squad car, then pointed out the knife. The police officer slipped on latex gloves and picked it up gingerly. "Been a long time since I saw one of those. They're illegal."

When the two police cars finally drove off, Walker pulled her against him. She wrapped her arms around him and held him tightly.

"I don't believe that happened," she said into his chest. "People don't get mugged in Otter Tail."

"God. What if you'd been alone?" He buried his face in her neck. "I wanted to kill him."

"They just wanted to scare me." She tried to sound confident, but her voice wobbled.

He cupped her face in his hands. "You really believe that?"

"I don't know," she said, closing her eyes and burrowing closer. Rusty had looked as if he did want to hurt her. As if he looked forward to it.

"You shouldn't walk home from work anymore."

"I know. I'll drive from now on."

"I'll take you and pick you up. Just in case someone is waiting in the parking lot." Anger glittered in his eyes and his jaw worked. "Nothing's going to happen to you, Jen."

A gust of wind blew past the corner, and she tugged her sweater more tightly around her. "They followed us out of the Harp." Her teeth chattered, and she was suddenly freezing.

"Yeah. They were waiting for you to leave." He took off his coat and wrapped it around her. "Let's get you home."

He tucked her close, and she leaned against him.

"You were so fast." She'd barely seen him move.

He took a deep breath, and some of the tension left his shoulders. "Working on the boat was good for something, I guess. One of my jobs was breaking up fights on the charters. It didn't take long to figure out what worked."

"Fights? On fishing boats?"

"Alcohol, testosterone and competition. Never a good mix."

"Oh, Walker."

Another thing to lay at her door.

CHAPTER SIXTEEN

"I HAVEN'T TASTED SALMON in a long time," Walker said to Jen as they sat around the dinner table the following Monday. "It was…good."

"Right," she answered, a smile tugging on her mouth.

"Jen! You could be more gracious," her mother scolded.

"You're right, Mom." She turned to him. "Thank you, Walker. It's so kind of you to say so. Your praise makes me giddy with joy."

"Smart-ass," he said under his breath.

Everyone was talking at once. Nick and Stevie were chattering about something that had happened at school that day, and Adam and Tommy were arguing about the video game they'd been playing earlier. Jen sat next to Walker, and she'd given up trying to inch away every time her leg bumped his. Her parents beamed at them from their seats at either end of the dining-room table.

The chaos was comfortable.

"Walker, you are gonna kick ass tomorrow night," Nick crowed, snapping him out of his trance.

"Nick," his grandmother said, her smile disappearing. "That's not appropriate language for the dinner table."

Walker cleared his throat. "Uh, thanks, Nick. You've been a big help getting *Sorceress* ready."

He shrugged, but Walker could practically see his chest swell. "I'll probably be able to get extra credit from my programming class."

Walker had been surprised how much help Nick had contributed. He'd done good work and had learned fast. The kid was talented. "Let me know if you need a note or something."

"Sure."

Stevie elbowed him, but Nick pretended he hadn't noticed. Before Walker could say anything more, Tommy and Adam demanded that he settle their argument about the video game.

By the time Jen and her mother signaled the kids to clear the table, he felt as if he'd been having dinner with them for years.

He carried his plate into the kitchen, and when Nell Horton went back to the dining room, he said to Jen, "Thanks again for inviting me." He nudged her hip with his. "To eat the fish we caught together."

"I had nothing to do with catching those fish. And you know I thought you'd refuse."

"Is this what it's always like?" He gestured to the other room, where the kids were still talking.

"Unfortunately, no. If you want the complete experience, you're welcome to join us when Nick is sulking and sarcastic and Tommy is whining."

"No, thanks," Walker said. "I'll keep my illusions."

"Homework time, guys," Jen called.

The four headed for the basement without an argument, and Jen narrowed her eyes.

"What?" he asked.

"They agreed to that way too quickly." She called down the stairs, "I'm coming to check on you, and there better not be any horsing around."

"Horsing around?" Nick's voice floated up to her. "What's that?"

"Remember, I'm listening."

"I talked to CPS today," Nell said quietly. "They think they have a foster home for Stevie and Adam. I said they were welcome to stay here for now."

"Thanks, Mom, but they should probably go to a foster home, anyway. Stevie and Adam are assuming they'll go home once their parents are out on bail, but they may not be allowed to go back there. That would be terribly upsetting for them, and they'll need to be with a family who knows how to care for them in that complicated situation."

"Those Meltons don't deserve such sweet children."

"No, Mom, they don't. But we have to deal with the reality, not what we want things to be."

Jen shifted her gaze to Walker, then quickly looked away.

"Do you want coffee, Walker?" Nell said with a smile as she noticed him standing there. Apparently she hadn't noticed the sudden tension.

"No, thanks," he said easily. "I have a lot to do before we launch the game tomorrow night." He glanced at Jen. "Walk me to the door?"

"Take your time, honey," Nell said, squirting dish detergent into the sink. "Your dad and I will be in here for a while."

"Mom," Jen said under her breath. "Knock it off."

Biting back a smile, Walker waited until they were on the screened porch to say, "She's not very subtle, is she?"

"She doesn't know the meaning of the word. Sorry."

"It's kind of funny." He ran his fingers down Jen's arm. "Are you going to be at the Harp tomorrow?" he asked.

186 CAN'T STAND THE HEAT?

"Of course. I'm working."

"Think your boss would let you out of the kitchen for a while?" He wanted her to see his work. And wasn't that pathetic? It was as if he were a kid again, waiting for his crush to notice him.

"I wouldn't miss it." She put her palm on his chest, and his heart jumped. "Nick is so excited about this. Thank you for making him feel special."

"He *is* special." Walker put his hand over hers.

"He's been his old self again," she said, cupping Walker's face. "I suspect it was a lot of extra work for you, but it was so good for Nick. Especially since…" She clamped her mouth shut.

"Since what?"

She shook her head.

"You can't leave me hanging," he said, drawing her closer. "Tell me."

Sadness flickered in her eyes. "Tony and Nick fight a lot."

"About what?"

She smiled, but it looked strained. "Oh, everything. You'd know exactly what I was talking about if you had a—"

Her eyes widened. "If I had a what, Jen?" he asked slowly. "If I had a child? A son of my own?" Carefully, he let go of her and took a step away.

"Nick's not—"

"He's not my son. I get it. Good night, Jen." Without a backward glance, he was gone.

THE NEXT NIGHT, Jen could hear the buzz of anticipation in the Harp all the way from the kitchen. The pub had been packed since the doors opened, and now it was so crowded that people could barely move. She'd sent out the last order, and was looking around to check that she'd cleaned everything.

She was dragging her feet, she realized.

She had to make a decision about the paternity test, and soon. Once Walker showed his game, he'd have no reason to stay in Otter Tail.

It was the right thing to do. And the idea made her sweat.

She threw the sponge into the sink. "Damn it."

Nick poked his head into the kitchen, his eyes bright. "Come on, Mom. Walker's just about ready."

"I'll be right out," she said, struggling to smile. "Two minutes."

"Okay." He glanced over his shoulder. "Maddie said to tell you she's saving you a stool at the bar."

"Are you going to sit with us?"

He rolled his eyes. "Duh. I'll be with Walker."

How would Nick feel if it turned out that he was really Walker's son?

He'd be confused. Shaken. Upset. In spite of his

battles with Tony, he knew his father loved him. What would happen to their relationship?

She wouldn't think about it tonight. Right now she was going to enjoy watching the game and savor the knowledge that her son had a role in getting it ready.

When she slid onto the seat next to Maddie, her friend held up a small black box. "Walker gave me one of the controllers," she said. "You want it?"

"God, no. I wouldn't know what to do with it. Give it to someone who plays video games." Augie Weigand was standing at the end of the bar, looking hungrily at the boxes four other patrons held. "Hey, Aug. Use this one."

Augie's face lit up. "Thanks, Jen." He ran his fingers over it, testing the buttons and the joystick.

Ian Hartshorn elbowed him. "Give you twenty bucks for it."

"No way, man."

"What do you know about this game?" Maddie handed Jen a beer.

"Not a thing. When Nick and Tommy talk about gaming, my eyes glaze over."

"Yeah, I never got the appeal of sitting in one spot and staring at a TV for hours," Maddie said cheerfully. "But it's great for the Harp. And Walker is going to leave the system and a bunch of games, too. We can have regular tournaments." She nodded toward the door. "Hey, look, Tony's here."

Her ex had just walked in, and Jen almost wanted to kiss him. Nick would be thrilled that his father was taking an interest in what he did. "Nick must have told him about helping Walker with the game."

"He's making an effort," Maddie said, apparently reading her mind. "That's great."

"Yeah." It was good that Tony was trying with Nick. Really, it was. But sometimes it would be easier if Tony had been a complete jerk with his sons and they could simply cut him out of their lives.

As Nick and Walker fussed with a machine, Maddie asked quietly, "What's going on with you and Walker?"

"Nothing." Jen's face burned, and she tried to hide it by drinking her beer.

"Really? Your kid helps him with the game. You blush when I ask about him. But there's nothing going on?"

"Okay, maybe he wants there to be something." And so did she. "But he reminds me of the person I used to be. And I don't want to be that girl anymore. I don't even want any reminders. I was so horrible to him."

"You can move beyond that," Maddie said softly. "Look at me."

"What I did to Walker is a lot more than a bunch of kids teasing each other."

Maddie narrowed her eyes. "When you and Delaney were helping me plot revenge on Quinn, you mentioned something that you'd done in high school. Something bad. Was that Walker?"

"Yes." She shifted on her seat, trying to find a way to change the subject.

A blast of trumpet music from the speaker drowned out Maddie's response, and a picture of an enormous castle appeared on the screens. Lightning crackled above the gray stone building, and clouds swirled around the turrets. Mist rose from the ground, curling up the walls.

A sword appeared on the screen, and then lifelike images of four young men walking up to the castle door. It creaked open and they stepped inside.

A flash of light appeared at the top of the staircase, and a woman materialized out of it. She was tall and blond and wore a black leather bustier, tall leather boots and the world's skimpiest black leather bikini bottom. Her face was indistinct.

"Who dares to intrude?" she asked.

She started down the stairs, and her face slowly swirled into focus. Jen shifted uncomfortably. The sorceress looked a lot like her. Hazel eyes, mouth and nose…she could be looking in a mirror.

The crowd in the pub stirred. "That's Jen," a man said loudly. Everyone swiveled to look at her.

When the sorceress reached the bottom of the stairs, she turned to one of the four characters. A tattoo of a sun and moon, twined together, peeked out from the edge of her bikini.

Jen gasped. The sorceress's tattoo was almost identical to hers. Only two men knew that tattoo was there.

One of them was Walker.

Her glass wobbled as she set the beer on the bar. Maddie turned to her. "Jen? Tell me you don't have a tattoo on your butt."

She ignored her friend as she stared at the screen. The leather-clad woman raised her arm. Light and smoke flew from her fingertips, and one of the men tumbled over. A lightning bolt quivered in his chest, right where his heart would be.

"Leave my house," she said, turning to the other characters. "Before you meet the same fate as your friend." She snapped her fingers and disappeared in a flash of smoke.

The game went on, with the three men, joined by the recovered fourth, scouring the castle for signs of the sorceress. She shot lightning bolts at them, changed them into dogs, set traps for them. Jen was numb. Walker had made her the villain of his game.

She felt people watching her, but she focused on the screen. The picture was wavy and blurred, but she refused to let the tears fall.

Out of the corner of her eye, she saw Walker weaving through the crowd. Toward her. She looked around frantically, but there was nowhere to go. Too many people, packed too closely together. She was trapped.

"Jen, I'm sorry," he said in a low voice. "I didn't realize—"

"Go away, Walker. You're making it worse," she said without looking at him.

He hesitated, and she kicked him in the shin. "Go. Away."

As he backed off, she wanted to run out of the Harp, crawl into a hole somewhere and stay there for about a hundred years. Far from Otter Tail.

As the game progressed, every time the sorceress appeared on the screen people glanced at her. Comparing. Wondering.

Tony's gaze burned into her, and her stomach twisted. He would have figured out how Walker knew about that tattoo.

By the time the sorceress had been vanquished and the screen faded to black, Jen was shaking with humiliation. Her face was hot and she wanted to squirm. But she made herself sit perfectly still.

Her hand cramped, and she realized she was clutching her beer glass. Setting it carefully on the bar, she stared blindly at the logo for GeekBoy, Walker's company, on the screen.

Walker had made her the villain in a video game that millions of people would see. Starting right here in Otter Tail.

She *had* been the villain in his life.

She'd embarrassed him publicly, all those years ago. Humiliated him.

Maybe she deserved to be a villain in his game.

Maybe now they were even.

"That's not my mother." Nick's voice rose above the crowd. "It didn't look anything like her. And she doesn't have a tattoo. Right, Mom?"

CHAPTER SEVENTEEN

WHEN JEN DIDN'T ANSWER, Nick repeated, "You don't have a tattoo, Mom. Right?"

Did she want Nick to see his mother run away? Refuse to face what she'd done?

What kind of example would that be?

She slid off the bar stool and pushed through the crowd toward the big plasma television Walker had installed. Nick was standing beneath it, his cheeks flushed, his leg jittering.

"Tell them, Mom."

She touched his shoulder, knowing he'd hate any public display of affection. "It's okay, Nick," she said quietly.

Taking a deep breath, she turned to face her friends. People she'd grown up with and known for years. Walker, white-faced, moved to intercept her. She ignored him.

"I'm sure you all think Walker used me as the model for Neoma." She dragged in a shuddering breath and tried to smile. "I don't know about that—she's way too hot to be based on me."

Nervous laughter rippled through the crowd, and people shuffled their feet. Jen put her hands behind her and grabbed on to the table for support. "But if that was me up on the screen, it would only be fair. Because I *was* the villain in his life. In high school."

"Jen, no," Walker said, elbowing his way toward her.

"Any of you who went to school with us know that Walker was expelled right before we graduated. It was my fault. I did something to him that I've been ashamed of ever since. And no, Hank," she said to the guitar player as he started to speak. "I'm not going to tell you what it was. That's between Walker and me."

Nick stared at her as if he didn't recognize her, and she couldn't bear to meet his gaze. At some point in every kid's life, he finds out that his parents aren't perfect. She swallowed hard. If Nick hadn't realized it before, he sure knew it now. If she allowed herself to think about his disappointment, his embarrassment, she *would* run away.

Get through the next two minutes. Then she could leave with a scrap of dignity.

"Walker tried to tell me he didn't realize Neoma was me, and I believe him." Did she? It didn't matter. This was her penance. She clenched her hands more tightly around the table and managed a wobbly smile. "But maybe I should ask him for residuals."

Laughter rippled across the room.

"Enjoy the game, everyone, and the system Walker donated to the Harp," she added. "We'll all remember his generosity long after he leaves."

She pushed her way back through the crowd, not meeting anyone's eyes. Refusing to stop. Until Tony appeared in front of her.

"Jen. How did—"

"Not now, Tony. Later."

Oh, God. He knew. She saw it in his tight jaw, the anger in his eyes.

She was almost at the door, her face still burning, when her mother put a hand on her arm. "We'll take Nick out for dinner," she said quietly. "We'll go get Tommy and pick up Stevie and Adam, too. Even though they were moved to the Fisks' today, we promised to let them know how the game turned out. We'll be gone for a while."

"Thanks, Mom," she said around the lump in her throat. "I'll tell you about it later."

"You don't have to, dear. It sounds as if you've paid for your mistake many times over."

Her mother's understanding, her gentle voice,

made the tears overflow. Jen didn't deserve her mother's kindness. Jen deserved exactly what Walker had done.

She put her head down as she hurried out the door. The evening was chilly, and she'd left her coat behind, but nothing could make her go back into the Harp.

When she reached her car, she realized she'd left her purse and car keys in the pub, too. She leaned her forehead against the roof, tears flowing faster, until she heard footsteps crunching over the gravel.

"Jen, wait."

Walker. She couldn't bear to look at him. She began to run. Her side ached and her lungs heaved, but she wouldn't stop.

He caught up as she reached her house. Stepping in front of her, he ran backward. Slowing her down. Forcing her to face him.

"Jen, please. Stop."

She slowed, then faltered to a halt. Dragging in deep breaths, she bent over, hands on her knees.

When she could speak, she said, "Why did you follow me?"

He stared at her, astonished. Bewildered. "Did you think I wouldn't? That I would let you walk out and not do or say anything?"

She wanted to step around him and finish her escape. But, just like at the Harp, some things were better faced immediately. "Why not?" she asked wearily.

"You can't believe I did that deliberately. That I put that game on the screen, knowing she looked like you."

Jen lifted one shoulder. "Kind of hard to miss, Walker."

"I haven't seen her for months." He closed his eyes and took a deep breath. "I mean, of course I have, but I didn't *see* her."

Sweat was drying on her skin, and she shivered. "I meant what I said at the Harp. I don't blame you. I owed you. Yes, it was humiliating, but I deserved it. I humiliated you in front of the whole school. But did you have to do it with Nick there? God! You think he's your son, but you still let him see that? Slap him with the knowledge that his mother had sex with you?"

"Do you really think I would do that? To you or Nick?"

She closed her eyes and wiped away the tears that had streamed down her face all the way home. Nick knew. Tony knew. What was next?

"You're cold. Let's go inside." He put his hand on her lower back and steered her up the steps, through the porch and into the living room. "How about some tea?"

This was her house. He wasn't going to take care of her in her own place. "I'm fine."

Walker stood stiffly in the center of the room, hands in his pockets, as if bracing himself for a blow. "Will you give me a chance to explain?"

She stayed out of his reach, hugging herself to stop the shaking. Because she was cold. That's all.

One side of his mouth curved. "A little intimidating," he murmured. "No wonder I thought of you when I created my kick-ass, take-no-prisoners character. I designed her a long time ago," he continued. "Before I had a game for her. Were you the model? Apparently so. But I swear, Jen, I didn't do it deliberately. Heck, I haven't thought about you for years." He reached for her hand, but she pulled it away. "Until I came back to Otter Tail."

"I get that you used me as your villain. But did you have to use the tattoo?" Her face burned as if she'd been slapped. "Everyone is going to realize…"

"No one's going to realize anything. It's a game, Jen. Make-believe. Of course she had a tattoo. It's part of her persona." He tucked a stray strand of hair behind her ear. "I'm so sorry. I'll change it before it goes public."

She studied his eyes and saw only remorse. Apology. There was no guilt in his clear gaze.

She doubted he was a good enough actor to hide that.

"All right, Walker, I believe you didn't do it on purpose. It was horribly humiliating, but now I know how you must have felt after...after I seduced you. When you were expelled. It doesn't feel good."

"I saw Tony stop you. What are you going to say to him?"

"Oh, God, I have no idea." She pressed her palms against her hot cheeks. "He knows. And from now on, every time we fight about something, he'll throw that at me."

"What happened, Jen? With you and Tony." Walker started to reach for her again, then dropped his hand. "Tell me about your marriage."

He had the right to ask. Her relationship with Tony was the reason she'd asked him to change that grade.

"He didn't ask me to sleep with you," she said in a low voice. "I never intended to. It just...got out of hand." She stared down, remembering the way she'd flirted with Walker. The painfully eager expression on his face. He'd been an earnest boy, serious and sweet. So different from cocky, confident Tony.

Back in high school, Walker would push his glasses higher on his nose when he was nervous. He'd pushed them up a lot that day. She remembered how his hand had shaken when she took it to lead him into that closet. The way he'd kissed her, as if she was infinitely precious.

"I never told Tony," she said.

"But now he knows."

"Yes. I'm such a hypocrite." She swallowed hard. "I betrayed him, too. If Nick isn't his son… We had a lot of problems, but he didn't deserve that."

"It was a crappy thing to do to him. But you weren't married to him when we had sex."

"I was in love with him. Committed to him. That's just as bad. I never even considered he wasn't Nick's dad…."

"How come you two didn't make it?"

She stared out the window, unseeing. "He lost his baseball scholarship when the principal found out what you'd done. So instead of college, he went straight to the minors. He traveled a lot. I was alone at home with a baby. Being married wasn't what either of us thought it would be."

"You were young."

"We made a lot of grown-up mistakes." She dropped onto the couch, curled her knees into her chest and wrapped her arms around them. "He blew out his rotator cuff, and that was the end of baseball. He got the job as a cop in Green Bay, but things were never the same.

"The final blow was probably as much my fault as his. He cheated on me. Neither of us was happy. He wasn't what I wanted, and I couldn't be what he wanted, either." She tugged at a loose thread on the couch cushion. "Everything came to a head one night when I got home early from a visit to my parents. Tommy was going to a birthday party the next day, and I didn't want to take a chance on traffic.

"It was late, close to midnight. Both the boys were asleep in the car. When I pulled up to the house, the lights were all on, so I knew Tony was there. I left the boys in the car and went in to get him. I wanted him to carry Tommy to bed so he wouldn't wake up."

Walker sat next to her, took her hands in his and uncurled her fists. Her nails were digging painfully into her palms. He smoothed them out, then twined his fingers with hers.

He let go of one of her hands and pulled her against his chest. His heart thumped beneath her ear, steady and strong. Reassuring.

"He was in my kitchen with a woman. Naked. Having sex on my table." Her throat closed. "I loved that kitchen. Loved everything about it. Cooking was the only time I was really happy." Jen took a deep breath, let it out slowly. "I'd found that table at a yard sale, spent hours stripping it, then refinishing it until it was perfect. And he was using it to bang some blonde with plastic breasts."

Walker wrapped his arms around Jen and rocked her while she cried, deep, wrenching sobs that tore at her throat and made her chest ache. By the time they slowed, his shirt was wet and she was drained. He rubbed her back while she hiccuped, and when she was sure she could talk without breaking down again, she pushed away from him.

"He betrayed me. But our marriage was over long before that."

"Why did you sleep with me?" he asked abruptly. "Back then."

She raised her head to look at him. "Truth?"

"Tell me."

"I wasn't planning that. But when you kissed me, touched me…" She cupped his cheek. "It had never been like that for me before. You were so tender. So careful with me. You made me feel cherished."

She let her hand fall away. "Afterward, I was so ashamed. I'd been using you, and you were loving me."

He brushed the tears from her cheeks. "You know I had a crush on you. Had for a long time. I thought I'd died and gone to heaven."

"Too bad it was really hell."

He smiled. "I wouldn't say that. Purgatory, maybe."

He pressed a kiss into her palm, and desire shuddered through her. Crazy to want him now. But she did.

Not just wanted him. She needed him to fill the empty places inside her. To make her feel whole again.

Before Walker had come back, she hadn't felt whole in a very long time.

CHAPTER EIGHTEEN

WALKER PRESSED A KISS into her palm, and just that small touch of his mouth made her tremble. "I want you, Walker."

He closed his eyes. "Can't do it, Jen. Not now."

"What?" Humiliated, she jumped to her feet.

"There's nothing I want more," he said fiercely. "But there are rules."

"What are you talking about? What rules?" She tried to tug her hand away, but he held on effortlessly.

"On top of everything else, you don't take advantage of a woman when she's fragile."

"You think I'm fragile? That I don't know what I want?" She yanked again, and he let her go.

"You're upset. You need to be comforted. And as much as I want you, Jen, I want it to be for the right reasons when we make love."

"You want some reasons? I lie in bed at night and think about you, Walker. About how I want to touch you. How I want you to touch me."

She stared at him, not caring that she'd made herself vulnerable. "I try to think of excuses to go to that motel you're staying in."

"You're making it hard to do the right thing, Jen." He held her gaze. "Almost impossible."

"*Almost* impossible?" She leaned in, lost in the need in his eyes, the heat pouring off his body and warming hers. "I'll have to work harder, then."

She'd never begged anyone to make love with her. What had happened to the woman who used to live in her body?

She'd fallen in love with Walker Barnes. Eventually, she'd grasp the irony of that fact.

Right now, nothing mattered besides Walker.

She tugged at his hand. "Come with me," she murmured.

"Jen," he groaned, his mouth over hers. "Are you sure?"

"I've never been more sure of anything." She swayed toward him, inhaled his scent, memorized the shape of his back, the curve of his hip, the way he gasped when she touched him.

He opened the buttons on her shirt before she realized what he was doing.

His hands were warm as he brushed the edges of the shirt away, revealing her bright pink bra. "I think

I have a new favorite color." He nuzzled the cleft between her breasts as he trailed his fingers over her.

"Take off your shirt," he said.

She let it slide to the floor, and he ran his hand over her stomach, her sides, her arms, her back, loosening her bra and sliding the straps down her shoulders.

He stared at her, before gently pulling the bra off and tossing it on the couch. "You're so beautiful," he whispered. "More beautiful than I remembered." He cupped her, then rubbed her nipples with his thumbs. She couldn't hold back her cry as she arched into him.

He picked up her discarded clothing and took her hand. "Where's your bedroom?"

"Upstairs." Her voice shook as she led him up there. She'd never bothered to get new furniture, and her dresser was scuffed and scratched. The mattress on the bed sagged in the middle, and the posters of Mel Gibson in *Braveheart* and Garth Brooks on stage were old and faded. It looked like a shrine to her high school days.

As if she'd been frozen in time since her senior year.

She turned into his arms and kissed him. "I'm not fragile or upset, Walker," she said, nuzzling his ear. "I want you." She took his hand and placed it on her bare breast, so he could feel her heart racing.

Then she locked the door and tugged his shirt out of his slacks. His muscles tensed and quivered when she touched him. When she opened his shirt and pressed her mouth to his muscled abdomen, he drew her against him.

"Mmm, good idea," he said, lowering his head to her stomach. As he teased her with his mouth, he unbuttoned her jeans and slid them down. She collapsed onto the bed.

His eyes darkened as he looked at her, wearing only sheer pink panties that matched her bra. "Turn over," he said, his voice hoarse.

She rolled onto her stomach, and he drew the elastic down and traced the tattoo on her hip. Then he pulled off the underwear and kissed that tattoo. "Sun and moon. Light and dark. I dreamed about this."

She looked over her shoulder, and he leaned up and kissed her. "I'm sorry about the game. I'll change the graphic before we release it."

"It's okay," she managed to say. "I'm not thinking about the game anymore." She rolled onto her back and reached for him.

Instead of following her onto the bed, he knelt between her legs and put his mouth on her.

"Walker," she cried as desire swamped her. In a few moments she was writhing against him, mindless with need, making sounds she barely recognized as her own.

She cried his name as a climax exploded through her, and he held her as the pleasure went on and on. Finally, when she was limp in his arms, he shoved off his clothes, rolled on a condom and slid into her.

They fit together perfectly, as she'd known they would. As they had in all her dreams. "Walker," she murmured as she held him tightly and wrapped her legs around him. "Love me."

"I am. I will." He buried his face in her neck. This time when she came, he was with her.

THE SOUND OF VOICES roused Walker, and he looked up, disoriented. Who was that?

He wasn't at the motel, he realized the next moment. He was curled around Jen, their legs entwined, his hand cupping her breast. In her bedroom.

He glanced at the clock. At midnight.

A door slammed in the distance, and she stirred. She smoothed her hand over his hip, then smiled at him. "I guess it wasn't a dream," she murmured as she kissed him.

He touched his fingers to her lips. "Shh. Your parents and the boys are home," he breathed into her ear. *The boys. Nick.* How could he have made love with her without telling her what he'd done? Without telling her he'd sent in that sample?

Her eyes widened and she grabbed his wrist. "Oh, God. We fell asleep. Did I lock the bedroom door? Oh, my God. I didn't."

"You did. I remember. Shh." His arms tightened around her. What if her parents found him here?

What if Nick did? What would he think?

Walker and Jen were adults. He didn't care what her parents thought.

Nick was a different story.

"Mom?" That was Tommy, calling up the stairs from the first floor.

"Hush, Tommy. She's asleep. You can talk to her in the morning," Jen's mother said.

"Go to bed, boys," Al added. "It's late and you have school tomorrow."

The kids' answers were indistinct. Finally, Walker heard them clattering down to their room in the basement.

He reached over Jen and switched off the lamp on the nightstand, then kissed her neck as they listened to her parents moving around on the first floor. When they started up the stairs, she tensed in his arms.

They lay still as the shadows of two sets of feet

passed Jen's bedroom. Moments later, the hall light went out and a door closed.

He let out his breath, and Jen shifted so she could murmur into his ear, "They read for a while before they go to sleep. You need to stay for another hour or so."

"That's going to be a real hardship," he said, stroking his palm down her back and over her hip. "I'm not sure how I'll hold up. I may have to distract myself."

She batted his hand away, but she was smiling. "I thought the game was bad, but this is *real* humiliation. To be thirty-two years old and caught in bed by my parents."

"We're not caught yet, but keep talking and we will be. I'll have to figure out a way to keep you quiet."

He kissed her again, drawing her lower lip into his mouth and sucking on it. She smiled, then giggled against his lips.

"What?"

"You don't think this is funny?" She buried her face in her pillow as her shoulders shook with laughter. "I should be worrying about Nick doing this. Not worrying about being caught doing it myself."

Nick. When Walker had begun pursuing Jen, it had been about Nick. He'd barely given the kid a thought tonight. Lying here, holding her, he couldn't think of anything but Jen. About how much he'd wanted her. How much he wanted her again. How he was afraid he'd never get enough of her.

To hide his uneasiness, he slid his leg between hers and touched her tattoo. "We have some time to kill," he whispered. "Any ideas?"

THE HOUSE WAS DARK and still hours later when he tiptoed down the stairs after Jen. She eased the front door open, and he followed her onto the screened porch, where the streetlight shining through the window turned the light robe she wore almost transparent. The curves revealed by the sheer cotton robe made him itch to burrow his hands beneath it and touch her again. Then he saw two school backpacks, carelessly dumped on the floor, and he put his hands in his pockets.

He had feelings for Jen, he realized uneasily. More than he'd imagined he would. It made him understand what he'd done. The miscalculation he'd made.

There were consequences to sending that sample in, consequences he hadn't cared about when he'd dropped it in the mail.

What he'd done, sending in that DNA test without her permission, was wrong. So wrong. He'd broken her trust. Even worse, he'd made love with her, without making it right.

He had to resolve this. He didn't think Jen had been playing games tonight. And he was afraid he hadn't been, either.

"Jen," he began in a low voice.

"My parents' bedroom is right above us. Do you want to get caught?" She leaned into him. "Are you some kind of exhibitionist?"

He kissed her again, then let her go. Reluctantly. He wanted to hold on to her. "I'll see you tomorrow."

He would tell her what he'd done.

It was time to stop playing games.

CHAPTER NINETEEN

WALKER FORCED HIMSELF to ask her out for dinner on her day off. She seemed thrilled with the invitation, and that only made him feel more guilty. And when she reached for his hand at the candlelit table at the nicest restaurant in Sturgeon Falls, and told him she was crazy about him, he felt like scum.

He bundled her away from the restaurant without coffee or dessert. Her knowing smile made him sick—she thought he was eager to be alone with her. He pulled the Porsche to a stop at the end of a dirt road at an abandoned cherry orchard. She looked around and smiled. Stars glittered between the trees and a chorus of spring peepers croaked in the distance. The faint smells of pine and water drifted through the air.

"Beautiful," she murmured. She reached for his hand. "Romantic."

"It seemed like a good place to talk."

She slipped off one of her heels and lifted her leg

over the gearshift to skim her toes down his shin. "I like talking."

The caress of her foot on his leg drained all the blood from his head. Without conscious thought, he put his hand on her knee, and her silky skin was warm beneath his fingers.

"What did you want to talk about, Walker?" Her toes moved up and down. Up and down. Then she caught the hem of his slacks and her foot pressed against his bare leg.

"Ah, what were we discussing at dinner?" *Focus.* He had to do this. Tell her what he'd done. But he was hard as steel, and all he could think about was how Jen would feel beneath him. Over him. Around him.

"My restaurant." She lifted her hand to the top button of her blue blouse.

"Right. Yes." He stared at her fingers, pale against the dark fabric, as she fiddled with the button.

It slipped out of its hole.

"Stoves," she said, her voice dreamy as she unbuttoned the second button. Her fingers slid down her chest to the next one. "What size I want."

"What's a good size?" he asked hoarsely as she trailed a finger over her bra.

"Big." The third button slid free. "Definitely big."

He swallowed.

Her blouse gaped wide as she undid the fourth button, and he saw black lace. His mouth dry, he said, "I said pink was my favorite color. I was wrong."

Her shadowed breasts were creamy in the moonlight. When she undid the last button, the silk blouse fluttered open to reveal the white skin of her abdomen.

He reached across the gearshift and dragged her against him. The heat of her skin burned him and he knelt on the seat, trying to get closer. "Let's not talk about restaurants anymore," he said into her mouth. "You're making me hungry."

"Did I distract you?" Her hands trailed through his hair and roamed over his back. "I'm sorry. I'll stop."

Her laugh reached deep inside him, grabbing his heart and holding tight. "I don't want you to stop." *Ever*.

She let her blouse flow down her arms as she reached for him. "Tiny car, Walker." Her eyes gleamed with laughter. With desire. "It's a challenge. Are you up to it?" He closed his eyes as she skimmed her fingers over his hard length. "Think we can make this work?"

"Jen…"

She pulled at his sleeves, making the envelope in his pocket crinkle.

"Stop, Jen. We need to talk."

"Isn't that what we're doing?" She opened one of the buttons on his shirt, then another.

He put his hands over hers, pressing them against his chest. Holding them still.

Some of the laughter faded from her eyes. "What's wrong?"

"Nick. The DNA test."

She sat back in the leather seat and pulled her blouse back on. Began to button it. The valley between her breasts was shadowed and mysterious. He knew her scent now, knew he'd smell jasmine if he kissed her there.

She watched him quietly. Her smile had disappeared, but her expression was still soft. Loving.

"You can do the test," she said. "I thought you were crazy until you showed me the baby picture of your father." She did up another button. "You were right. It looked just like Nick."

"Jen…"

She put her hand on his arm. "I was scared of what would happen if you were right. I still am. What am I going to tell Nick? And Tony? If you're Nick's father, everything will change. My relationship with my son will never be the same. Neither will his relationship with his father.

"No matter what that test shows, Tony is Nick's dad. He's the one who held Nick after he was born.

He's the one who read to him. The one who taught him to throw a baseball." She smiled. "Even though Nick didn't want to learn."

"I don't want to take Nick away from Tony. I just want to be part of his life, too."

"You already are," she said. "He thinks you walk on water. Every other sentence out of him begins with 'Walker says.' That won't change if the test is negative."

"Having Nick think I'm a cool guy is a lot different from having him know I'm his father."

"Yes. It is. So do the test. Let's find out."

The cowardly part of him wanted to forget about the envelope nestled in his pocket. It wanted to thank Jen, have her give him some hairs from Nick's brush and run the test all over again. She'd never have to know.

But he didn't want lies between them. Secrets. If he was to have anything more with her, it had to be built on the truth. And it had to start now.

"I hope you can forgive me, Jen."

"I already have. You were right to push me to test him. I'm sorry it's taken so long."

He closed his eyes. Pulling the envelope out of his coat pocket, he laid it on her lap. "I'm sorry."

She frowned as she picked it up. "What's this? 'Who's Your Daddy?' What's that?"

"A firm that does paternity tests. You send the samples in and they send you the results."

"Is this an application?"

"No. It's the results."

"Results? What...? How...?" She gazed at the white envelope, then slowly raised her eyes.

"The day Nick had that fight over Stevie, he got a bloody nose," Walker said, his voice flat. "I ended up with a wad of bloody tissues in my pocket, and I sent them off. I didn't think you would ever agree, and I wanted to know."

"You had no right," she whispered. Her fingers on the envelope tightened.

"I know that."

She threw the envelope at him. "He's my son. *My son.*"

JEN GAZED AT THE ENVELOPE lying in Walker's lap, bright in the pale moonlight. The drawing of a man holding a baby, a question mark where his face should have been, mocked her. Walker had known about this for a long time. When he'd kissed her on the porch. When he'd played *Sorceress* at the Harp.

When they'd made love.

"Has it all been a game, Walker? Romancing me? Getting me to fall in..." She would not say that.

Not tonight. Not ever. "Seeing how stupid with lust you could make me?"

"No! God, Jen. It's not like that at all. I made a mistake. I'm trying to make it right."

"You must have been laughing so hard at me." Her skin crawled with humiliation.

She hadn't realized how easily a heart could break.

"I *did* want you. Desperately. And I felt horrible afterward. Like I'd betrayed you."

"Because you did! Why didn't you tell me about your 'mistake' then? It was a big night for confession. You could have jumped in at any time."

"Because I was a coward," he said quietly. "I didn't want to face what I'd done."

"So you set up this evening instead. Were you softening me up for the big revelation?"

When he didn't deny it, a chill shuddered through her. She'd thought this date had been about romance. About falling in love. Instead, it had been about lies. "Were you, Walker?"

"Yes. No." He shoved his hand into his hair. "I was trying to find some privacy to tell you what I'd done."

"You let me seduce you again." She buttoned the rest of her blouse with jerky movements. "Did you get a kick out of that? Poor Jen, she's so desperate she can't even see that I despise her. Did you enjoy that?"

"Of course I didn't. I hate what I've done."

His voice washed over her like ice. "Not enough to tell me before tonight. You used my feelings for you to manipulate me, Walker. And you used me to get close to Nick. I'll never forgive you for that."

The scent of him filled the small space, rewinding too many memories. The two of them on the front porch. Beneath the tree at the miniature golf course. Giggling together in her bed.

Tears welled in her eyes, and she fumbled with the door. When she finally got it open, she threw herself out of the Porsche.

"Get in the car, Jen. Let's talk this out."

"I can't be in that car. That close to you." Leaving the door hanging open, she began walking away. She'd left her shoes in there, the fancy, expensive heels she'd bought for tonight. She'd thought they were sexy.

Tiny stones in the grass bruised her feet, but she wasn't about to ask him for her shoes. She'd asked him to make love with her.

And look how that had turned out.

HE WAS LOSING HER.

Walker leaped out of the car. He wanted to grab her and hold on until she forgave him. Until she understood that he would do anything to make this right.

If he touched her now, she'd probably punch him.

"I didn't have to tell you, Jen," he said, desperate to find the words that would force her to understand. "At least I told you what I'd done."

"You think that makes it better? I trusted you, Walker. With my son." She bit back a sob.

"Tell me what to do, Jen. Please."

"Tell me what it says."

"I don't know." He looked at the envelope in his hands. "I didn't open it." He put it in her hand and closed her fist around it.

Jen stood in the moonlight, staring at the envelope. She was beautiful. Strong. And so alone.

CHAPTER TWENTY

JEN REACHED INTO her purse for her car keys, and her fingers brushed against the envelope.

Just as they had every other time she'd put her hand into her bag. The crinkle of the paper made her want to cry.

She'd left it in her purse because she didn't want the boys or her parents to find it. Couldn't bring herself to open it yet. What if Tony wasn't Nick's father? Would she tell Nick? Or Tony, for that matter?

And Walker. Walker had a right to know whether Nick was his son.

The boys were going to stay with Tony in Green Bay this weekend. She would have time to figure out what to do.

In the meantime, she had an hour before her sons got home from school. She'd already made sure they had everything they needed for their weekend away, and she was heading to the store she'd rented to work on her restaurant. Her mother had promised to see the boys off so Jen wouldn't have to be there when Tony arrived.

Grabbing the bucket of cleaning products she'd gathered, she headed for the front door. Bottles of window spray and disinfecting soap gurgled, reminding her of all that needed to be done before she could open her business. Work was good. She could lose herself in the scrubbing, the polishing.

As she reached for the doorknob, the bell rang. She pulled the door open and saw her ex on the porch.

"Tony. What are you doing here so early?" Oh, God. She knew why he'd come.

"I wanted to talk to you. Alone. Before the boys got home from school."

She could close the door in his face, tell him to go away. But that would just postpone the confrontation. "Fine. Come on in."

He glanced at the bucket she held. "You in the middle of something?"

"I was going to work on the space I rented for my restaurant."

"You finally pulled the trigger on that? Good for you."

"Thanks." She set the bucket down and pushed it to the side with her foot. "What's up?"

"Walker Barnes. How did he know about your tattoo, Jen?

"It doesn't matter. You and I are divorced."

"Was it because you slept with him?"

"Not your business." She headed back into the house.

Thank goodness. Tony had assumed Walker knew about the tattoo because he'd seen it recently. Not back then.

She'd barely made it past the door when Tony took her wrist and turned her to face him. "He didn't design that game in the last few weeks. That means he saw the tattoo in high school. Were you sleeping with him then? Is that why he changed my grades?"

"Does it matter? It was a long time ago."

He held her gaze and dropped her wrist. "Yes, Jen, it matters. It matters a hell of a lot. It would explain some things to me."

"Like what?"

"Like why everything was different after we got caught."

"Of course it was different. You lost your scholarship, so you couldn't go to college. I got pregnant, and we had to get married right away. When you signed up with that minor-league team, it meant you were on the road a lot. At training camps. We hardly saw each other." She nudged the bucket with her toe, unable to look him in the eye. "Of course things were different."

"I know I wasn't a perfect husband. Or a perfect father. But I've always thought it was my fault, you know? We couldn't go to college because I asked you to get Walker to change my grade, and I lost my scholarship. I wasn't around much when Nick was a baby." Tony clenched his jaw. "Maybe if there was a reason for the tension between you and me back then, I wouldn't feel like such a failure as a husband and a father."

"If you could blame Walker for it, you mean?"

"You don't think you have any blame there? If you were having sex with Barnes? If you were screwing around on me, maybe everything that happened wasn't my fault."

Had Tony been carrying around this guilt ever since Nick was young? Jen wondered. So many repercussions from that one mistake.

"Sit down, Tony." She waited until he'd settled on the couch. "No more lies. Yes, I slept with Walker. Once."

He jumped up from the couch. "I knew it. You cheated on me with that son of a bitch!"

She closed her eyes. "I was flirting with him, trying to get him to hack into the computer. To change your grades. Teasing, joking. It went a little too far."

"Is that what you call it? Going a little too far? For God's sake, Jen. We were a couple. You said you loved me."

"I did love you. I was desperate to help you. Even if it meant having sex with Walker. That's why everything was different afterward. I betrayed you, and I...I had a hard time with the guilt. You should have told me, Jen. Back then."

"Yes. I should have. But I was a corward."

Tony looked out the window. "What about Nick? Is he mine? I can count, you know. He was born nine months later. I've been wondering about that since I figured out how Barnes knew about the tattoo." He turned back to her. "That's a crappy thing to wonder about."

Her first instinct was to put him off. To avoid the confrontation. But she was done lying. "I'm not sure. I never doubted it. But Walker thinks Nick might be his."

Tony shoved his hand through his hair. "What a frigging mess."

"I'm sorry, Tony." She hesitated. "If I had a DNA test, knew for sure who Nick's biological father was, is it going to change how you feel about him?"

"Hell, Jen, I don't know." He walked across the living room, picked up the framed collection of

Nick's school pictures and stared at them for a long time.

Finally, he put them back on the bookshelf. "He's my kid. He'll always be my kid," he said quietly. "Maybe it would explain why he hates sports. Even when he was little, he didn't want to play baseball. Or anything else."

"Nick has been difficult with you," she said over the lump in her throat. "It's his age. Nothing to do with you."

"Hell, I know that." He picked up one of Tommy's baseballs from the end table and squeezed his hand around it, as she'd seen him do so many times. "I thought I was going to the show. The big leagues." He mimed throwing a pitch. "That we'd always be in love. What a naive kid I was."

"You would have made it to the big leagues if you hadn't blown out your shoulder."

He rolled it a couple of times and set the baseball down. "Maybe, maybe not." He tried to smile. "I kill in the cops' softball league in Green Bay, though."

"You should take Tommy and Nick to one of your games this summer. They've never watched you pitch."

"We'll see." He jiggled the change in his pocket as he stood by the door. "So what happens next? Do I need to give a blood sample or something?"

"I don't know. I'll find out."

"Okay." He picked up a picture of the two boys, studied it, then set it back in place. "I need to get out of here. Away. I'll be back when the boys are home from school."

"All right." She put her hand on his arm as he started to leave. "Thank you," she said quietly. "I'm glad everything is out in the open. And I'm sorry you always felt as if our breakup was your fault. I was as much to blame as you were."

He smiled wearily. "Maybe not quite as much. You didn't have sex with Walker on the kitchen table in front of me."

JEN PULLED INTO the lot of the Bide-A-Wee Motel and parked next to Walker's dark blue Porsche. She couldn't use the excuse he wasn't here, and run home.

No, she'd face him now. She had a lot that needed to be said.

When she knocked, she heard the scrape of a chair across carpet. Footsteps. He opened the door.

"Jen. What are you doing here?"

"I need to talk to you, Walker. May I come in?"

He stood to the side and swung the door wider.

The room was spartan, but spotless. It held a double bed, a small table, two chairs and a television. Walker's laptop was open on the table, with papers spread out next to it.

"You were working. I'm disturbing you."

"Of course you're not." He closed the lid of the computer. "Do you want to sit down?"

"I don't know." She retreated as far from him as she could get. "I have some things I need to say. First of all, I want to apologize."

He held up his hand. "No. You were right. It was a rotten thing to do to you, and I deserved all of your anger. Everything you said."

Some of the tension left her shoulders. "I should have let you do the DNA test as soon as I saw those pictures of your father. I knew they looked like Nick. I was just…" She bit her lip, determined not to let him see her cry. "I didn't want to face what I'd done. What we'd done. The possibility that Nick was your son. It was easier to deny everything."

"So what changed your mind?"

"Tony. He's taking the boys to Green Bay for the weekend, and he came early to talk to me. He wanted to know about the tattoo. How you knew about it. So I told him. He asked me if Nick was his son."

"What did you tell him?"

"That I didn't know. But he has a right to find out. And so do you." She pulled the envelope out of her purse. "So open this. I want to know, too."

WALKER REACHED FOR the envelope, but kept watching Jen. Her face was pale and she looked thinner. As if she hadn't eaten in the past five days. He wanted to wrap his arms around her and take away her pain, but he'd forfeited the right to hold her.

The envelope was wrinkled. One corner was bent, and there was a brownish stain on it. Where had she kept it? Had she thrown it away, then rescued it from the garbage?

He rubbed his fingers on the cheap paper, picked at a spot on the flap where the glue was coming loose.

"I thought you'd tear it open," Jen said.

He'd planned to. But if he opened this letter, and it said he wasn't Nick's father, that was the end. Jen would leave, and she wouldn't come back.

He glanced at the dresser drawer where he'd stashed the Ernie Banks baseball card for Tommy and the new computer for Nick. All he'd leave behind were two *things*.

He didn't want that. He wanted a life with Jen and Nick and Tommy. He wanted a family, with all the noise, messiness and turmoil that came along with it.

"What if I don't open this?" he said, tossing it onto the bed. "What if I throw it away and promise not to ask you about testing again. Would you give me another chance, Jen? I know I screwed up. I want a chance to make it right." He took a step closer to her. "I *need* a chance."

She shook her head. "Tony needs to know, too. And so do I."

Reaching in the envelope again, he slid his finger beneath the flap and pulled out the single piece of paper it contained. His heart pounded as he opened it. Scanned it.

Found his answer.

CHAPTER TWENTY-ONE

HE STARED AT THE PIECE of paper that had just changed his life.

"Walker? What does it say?"

He handed her the sheet. "It's a match. High probability that the subjects are related."

"Oh, my God."

He looked up to see the shock on her face. The paper fluttering to the floor.

He bent and scooped it up, checking again to make sure he hadn't misread it. Nick was his son. He had a child.

After the first surge of joy, Walker panicked. Nick lived two hundred and fifty miles away from him. He didn't want to be that far away from him. *His son.*

He'd fly up here regularly. He could do that. Hell, he might as well make that company jet pay for itself.

Maybe Nick could come to Chicago once in a

while, too. There was plenty of room in the condo. He could have one of the spare bedrooms. Do whatever he wanted with it.

Walker would see Jen frequently. Talk to her. She was the mother of his son.

Could this persuade her to give him another chance with her?

God, he was such a jerk. He'd just found out he had a kid, and he was wondering how he could use that information to get her back. The woman he loved.

Jen was staring at him, her hand over her mouth, and he dropped onto the bed. She hated him. Would she let Nick go to Chicago? Would she even allow Walker be a part of Nick's life?

What was she thinking?

"Jen. Say something."

Her eyes were huge in her ashen face. A face pinched with pain. And fear. "I thought it would be negative," she whispered. "Even after I saw the pictures, deep down I believed you were wrong. How could I not know the father of my child? How was that possible?"

"We all see what we expect to see," he answered.

"You didn't. You saw him once and you suspected."

"I was thinking about my father at the wedding

reception, knowing I had to stop by his grave before I left town. Dreading it. Then Nick smiled, and he was the image of my dad. If he hadn't smiled, if I hadn't been looking at him at that exact moment, it might never have occurred to me."

She sank onto a chair. "I should have wondered about it when I found out I was pregnant. I should have at least considered that you might be the father. But I didn't. And I stole fifteen years of his life from you."

"There's another way to think about it. What if you had told me Nick was my son? If I'd had a child to support, I never would have gotten off that fishing boat. I would have been miserable. I couldn't have taken a chance with my game, couldn't have started GeekBoy.

"Would I rather have had the time with Nick? I'm pretty sure I would make that trade. But we can't go back."

He picked up the white photo album he'd found stored with his parents' possessions. "I should have reconciled with my dad before he died." He opened the album, touched the baby picture that looked so much like Nick. "I should have made an effort. But I didn't."

Finally he turned to face her. "You didn't know you were keeping my son from me. I want to put that behind us."

A tear dripped down her cheek. "You have a lot more to forgive me for. What I did to you in high school changed your life. How do you get past something like that?"

"Yeah, you did a lousy thing. But it worked out for me in the end. I love my job. I have fun with it. Not to mention buckets of money. The lousy thing you did turned out to be pretty damn lucky for me."

He took a step toward her, then stopped. God, he wanted to do this right. Make sure he didn't ruin everything. "Why did you come here today, Jen? You could have opened the letter and then dropped it off. Put it in the mail. You didn't have to see me. To give it to me in person."

A tear rolled down her other cheek. "Tony and I talked, and I realized that the choices I made in high school were part of the reason our marriage failed. Stupid not to see that before, but it was easier to blame him. So I asked myself if I wanted to let another bad choice ruin whatever you and I might have."

"And what was your answer?" He gripped the edge of the desk to keep from reaching for her.

She took a deep breath. "I...I care about you, Walker."

He reached for her then, but she held her hand up. "No, I have to get this out. You're important to me, and that trumps a mistake you made. We'll need to…to see each other a lot. There are details to work out. You need a chance to get to know Nick. Spend time with him." Her eyes filled with tears again. "We have to tell him. Together, Walker. We'll tell him together."

He took her hands. "Could you maybe let me get a word in here?"

She sniffed and extracted her hands from his to dig a tissue out of her purse. "I'm sorry. I'm babbling."

"I love your babbling. In fact, I love everything about you, Jen."

The hope that filled her eyes was almost painful in its intensity.

"I didn't fall in love with Nick. I fell in love with you."

She threw herself into his arms. "I love you, too, Walker."

He folded her against him and closed his eyes. This was where he belonged. With Jen. Holding her. Loving her. Making a life with her.

"I have a lot to learn about loving someone," he said.

"So do I, Walker. I did a really bad job of it the last time." She cupped his cheek, loved the feel of his rough beard against her hand. "Maybe we can learn together."

"I'd like that. But it's going to take me a long time, I'm afraid."

"You think so?" She leaned back, studied him. Relaxed when she saw the twinkle in his eyes. "A year, maybe? Two?"

He ran his fingers up her side, over her ribs. "Fifty or sixty years. Maybe more. Do you think you can give me that much time?"

"Is that all? I was thinking more like forever. It'll take at least that long."

"Then we better get started."

He kissed her again, and she sighed into his mouth. "I love you, Walker."

His lips lingered on hers. "I thought I'd never kiss you again. Never hold you," he murmured. He nuzzled the side of her neck, and she sucked in a breath. "Never finish what you started in the car that night."

"I felt like such a fool."

"I'm so sorry I made you feel that way." He nipped at her earlobe. "Because it was the sexiest thing I've ever seen." He kissed her neck as he slid one hand up her arm, lingered at the bra strap on her shoulder. "What color are you wearing today?"

"Hmm. Let's find out." She undid the top button of her blouse, then looked down. "It's a plain red one. Hardly any lace at all. Small, too. Barely covers my nipples."

"You are a devil, Jen Summers." Grinning, he lifted the blouse over her head without bothering to unbutton it. When her hands got trapped as she tried to get it off, he eased her onto the bed. "Now this has definite possibilities. You're helpless. I can do whatever I want with you."

She squirmed beneath him, laughing as he kissed his way from her neck to the top of her breast. Then he looked up and their eyes locked. His smile faded. Hers did, too.

"Jen." He pulled her blouse the rest of the way off. When he kissed her again, she tasted his desperation. And her own.

He worshipped her body, and she worshipped his. He held her face as he kissed her, and she didn't look away. Couldn't. She saw the love in his eyes, and the promise. Whatever happened, they were one.

"You're part of me," he said as he slid inside her. "Always. And I'm part of you. Together, there's nothing we can't do. Don't ever forget that."

"Yes. Together," she murmured as she rose up and began moving.

He drove her higher, and she drove him. And when they fell, they fell together.

IT WAS MUCH LATER, and dark outside the motel room, when Walker pressed a kiss to her head and sat up. "So when do we tell Nick?"

She didn't want to open her eyes. Didn't want to surface from the sensual magic they'd created. But he was right. It was time to face the real world. So she sighed and sat up.

"I have to tell Tony first. Then we'll all talk to Nick together."

"Is he…is Nick going to be okay with this?"

She hesitated. "Probably not at first. He's a teenager, trying to figure out who he is. And we're going to tell him, hey, your dad isn't really your father. This other guy is."

"Is he going to hate me?"

"Maybe. But he'll hate me more." Nick was old enough to realize that she'd slept with both Tony and Walker. What a humiliating, painful thing to reveal to your son.

"He's not going to hate you," Walker said.

She sighed as she kissed him. He had a lot to learn about being a parent.

CHAPTER TWENTY-TWO

"WHAT THE HELL ARE YOU talking about?" Nick looked from her to Tony to Walker, confused and angry.

"This is a shock. You're upset. But Walker is your father," Jen repeated quietly.

Nick turned to Tony, who was leaning against the wall by the door. As if he wanted to run, but couldn't. "What kind of crap is that, Dad?"

Tony stared at Walker, and the living room seemed barely big enough to contain his anger. But Tony managed to control it. "Just what she's saying. Barnes is your biological father."

"That's total crap."

Tony pressed his lips together. "It's true, Nick."

Nick looked from her to Walker. She saw the exact moment when he got it. "You mean you, like, had sex with him? Before I was born?"

"Yes, Nick. I did. We did."

"And you let Dad think I was his kid?"

"No. I thought Dad *was* your father. It didn't occur to me that he wasn't."

Nick jumped up from the chair and shoved a hand through his hair. His fingers trembled as his gaze swung from Walker to Tony, then back to her. "So what you're saying is you were a skank in high school."

"Nick!" Tony erupted from his spot at the wall. "Apologize to your mother. And don't you say anything like that to her again. You treat her with respect."

"Respect? What do you think she'd say to me if I slept with a bunch of girls and got one of them pregnant? Huh?" He sneered. "What about all those lectures about saving myself and safe sex and that shit? I guess they didn't mean squat."

Jen pulled her son close. He resisted, holding his body stiffly away from hers. "I meant every word of what I said. I wanted you to learn from my mistakes. Be the kind of person I should have been." She rubbed his back. "The kind of man your dad is. And Walker."

When Nick raised his head, he had tears in his eyes. "You just said he's not my dad."

"I didn't say that." She looked over at Tony. *Jump in here. Any time.*

Tony came farther into the room. His hand hovered over Nick's shoulder and finally settled on it.

"You'll always be my kid," he said roughly. "No matter what that piece of paper says."

Nick pushed Jen away and turned to Tony. He hesitated, then reached for him. Tony folded his arms around him and rocked him from side to side. As he had when Nick was a baby. The boy's shoulders were shaking, and she heard the catch of a sob he tried to muffle.

"What about Tommy?" Nick finally said.

"What about him?" she asked.

"Is he, like, still my brother?"

"Of course he is." She tried to caress Nick's head and froze when he jerked away.

"Are you going to tell him?"

She let her hand drop. "It's up to you if and when we tell Tommy. But secrets always end up hurting more than the truth."

Nick looked at Walker. He took a step back, so he was standing next to Tony. "I don't care what you did with my mother back then," he said. "I already have a father."

Jen took Walker's hand, and he gripped hers tightly. "I know you do," he said. "Tony will always be your dad. I just…just want to be part of your life, too."

Nick stared at him. "What am I supposed to call you?"

"How about Walker?"

Nick lifted one shoulder. "Whatever."

"I know we dumped a load on you today, Nick," Tony said gruffly. "You want to go to B-Dubs? Get some wings?"

"No. I want you all to leave me alone." He spun around, pushed past Tony and took the stairs two at a time down to the basement. She heard another sob just before his door slammed shut.

The three adults froze, avoiding one another's eyes. Tony finally said, "Should I go down there?"

"Leave him for now," Jen answered. "He needs time to process all of this."

"I'll come back tomorrow." Tony stared hard at Walker. "We share him. You got that?"

"Yeah. I do."

Tony slammed the door on the way out, and the sound reverberated in the silent room. Walker was gazing at the stairs.

"It's going to be all right," Jen told him.

"How? He hates me."

"He doesn't hate you. We've shaken his whole world. Nothing is what he thought it was. Of course he's upset."

"I shouldn't have done the test. Shouldn't even have asked you to consider it."

"We had to do it. We had to face all the secrets, the lies, the silence of the past. We had to face the truth."

Walker waved toward Nick's room. "He's my son. *Our* son. How could I hurt him like this?"

"It wasn't just you," she said. "It was all of us."

"Is that supposed to make it easier? Because it doesn't."

He stepped toward the basement stairs, and she caught his hand and drew him back into the living room. "Going down there now will make him more upset," she said. But she wanted to run down there herself and gather Nick close. To protect him from all possible pain, as she'd done when he was a baby.

"I had no idea that being a parent could hurt so much." Walker wrapped his arms around her and held her tightly. "God, Jen, how do you do it?"

"One day at a time," she said. "That's how. Tomorrow will be better. So will the day after that. This is just the beginning."

Six months later

JEN SLID THE LAST PLATE onto the warming table and stepped away from the stove. The aroma of garlic and butter lingered in the air as one of her waitresses scooped it up and carried it into the dining room. As she went out, Walker walked into the kitchen.

"Have I ever told you you're beautiful when you're cooking?"

"Nope. You've never said that." Exhausted, she leaned against him and he dropped a kiss on her hair. "No one's died out there yet?"

"Nothing but raves. Come on out and accept your kudos."

It was the grand opening of the Summer House, and they'd invited their families and close friends to join them for dinner. Every table was full.

Quinn and Maddie sat with Delaney, Hank and Paul, and Stevie and Adam Melton were at a larger table with their foster parents and Dave and his family.

Walker's friend Kirit had flown in from Chicago with his family.

Everyone who was dear to her and Walker had joined them.

The linen tablecloths were blindingly white. Soft light from the wall sconces filled the room with a golden glow. The paintings on the walls, all done by local artists, complemented the clean, simple lines of the furnishings that Delaney had built—the serving counters, the cupboards, the host desk.

Everything was exactly as she'd imagined it would be. Hoped it would be.

Including her family.

Nick and Tommy sat with Tony and her parents. Nick was waving his hands, obviously trying to explain to Tony the computer project he was doing for Walker, and Tony was listening carefully and nodding. But it was clear from the puzzled expression on his face that he didn't understand what Nick was telling him.

He was trying, though. Tony had finally realized he couldn't force Nick to be the child he wanted, and was learning to appreciate his son for who he was.

Tommy was chattering to his grandparents, probably about baseball, judging from the equally blank look on her mother's face.

They were still working out the kinks, and probably would be for a long time, but after a stormy couple of months, Nick had begun to come to terms with having two fathers. Even more important, he'd realized that he wasn't being disloyal to one when he spent time with the other.

Walker put his arm around Jen's shoulder and tucked her close as she studied her restaurant.

Her dream.

Happiness bubbled through her like champagne. *My place. My town. My kids.*

My man.

All of them supporting her.

"It's perfect," she murmured.

"You made it perfect." He bent to kiss her.

"I had a lot of help," she said. "From everyone in this room."

"But you put it all together. You took the steps to make your dream come true."

He had, too, Walker realized.

He had everything he could want. The woman he adored. The son he loved more than life. A stepson he loved just as much.

He was a lucky, lucky man.

The hum of conversation faded as people gradually noticed them standing near the kitchen door. Jen cleared her throat, suddenly nervous, and Walker let her go, took her hand and squeezed gently.

"Thank you for coming," she began. The crowd stilled and gave her their attention. "Every one of you."

Nick sat straighter in his chair as his mother gave a little speech, and Walker saw the piece of paper he held in his hand. Nick caught his eye, and Walker nodded once. Tugging on his necktie, Nick started to stand, but Tony stopped him and straightened the tie.

Jen finished up, saying, "I hope you enjoyed your dinner." As everyone clapped and cheered, Nick pushed his chair back. He stood waiting for the cheers to subside, his face red.

"Uh, I have something I'd like to say." He glanced at Walker again, and Walker mouthed, *"You can do this."* He had no idea what the boys planned to say. Neither did Tony, as far as he knew, although Tony had helped them pick out suits for the occasion.

"I wanted to say I think it's really cool, Mom, that you did this. That you, like, never gave up until you opened your own restaurant." He glanced down at the piece of paper again, and Walker's eyes stung. That was his kid. Becoming a man.

"You, uh, showed me and Tommy that anyone can have their dream, if they work hard enough. We want you to know we're proud of you."

Tommy nodded vigorously. Beside Walker, Jen put her hand over her mouth, and he wrapped his arm around her shoulders again.

"So when I'm an adult, I'm going to run my own computer company." Nick pointed his finger at Walker as if he was aiming a gun. "And it'll kick some GeekBoy ass, dude."

As everyone laughed and Nick sat down, Tommy jumped up. "And I'm going to play ball for the Brewers."

Jen rushed over to her boys and engulfed them both in a fierce hug. Shoulders shaking, she whispered in first Nick's ear, then Tommy's. Then she kissed each of them.

"She's crying, Nick," Walker heard Tommy say. "Awesome, dude."

As Walker watched them, it was as if the first hard couple of months when Nick had been so prickly faded away. As he watched his family, Walker's heart expanded until he was afraid it would burst. He never knew he could love so much. So completely.

He wished he'd been able to make peace with his father before he died. Wished that he'd known how to have a relationship with him, the kind of relationship he was working on with Nick. He would always mourn that loss.

But when Nick caught his eye over his mother's shoulder and smiled, Walker saw his father smiling at him. Loving him.

And he smiled back.

* * * * *

COMING NEXT MONTH

Available June 29, 2010

LARGER-PRINT BOOKS!

GET 2 FREE LARGER-PRINT NOVELS PLUS
2 FREE GIFTS!

HARLEQUIN
Super Romance

Exciting, emotional, unexpected!

YES! Please send me 2 FREE LARGER-PRINT Harlequin® Superromance® novels and my 2 FREE gifts (gifts are worth about $10). After receiving them, if I don't wish to receive any more books, I can return the shipping statement marked "cancel." If I don't cancel, I will receive 6 brand-new novels every month and be billed just $5.44 per book in the U.S. or $5.99 per book in Canada. That's a saving of at least 13% off the cover price! It's quite a bargain! Shipping and handling is just 50¢ per book.* I understand that accepting the 2 free books and gifts places me under no obligation to buy anything. I can always return a shipment and cancel at any time. Even if I never buy another book from Harlequin, the two free books and gifts are mine to keep forever.

139/339 HDN E5PS

Name _____ (PLEASE PRINT)

Address _____ Apt. #

City _____ State/Prov. _____ Zip/Postal Code

Signature (if under 18, a parent or guardian must sign)

Mail to the Harlequin Reader Service:
IN U.S.A.: P.O. Box 1867, Buffalo, NY 14240-1867
IN CANADA: P.O. Box 609, Fort Erie, Ontario L2A 5X3

Not valid for current subscribers to Harlequin Superromance Larger-Print books.

Are you a current subscriber to Harlequin Superromance books and want to receive the larger-print edition?
Call 1-800-873-8635 today!

* Terms and prices subject to change without notice. Prices do not include applicable taxes. N.Y. residents add applicable sales tax. Canadian residents will be charged applicable provincial taxes and GST. Offer not valid in Quebec. This offer is limited to one order per household. All orders subject to approval. Credit or debit balances in a customer's account(s) may be offset by any other outstanding balance owed by or to the customer. Please allow 4 to 6 weeks for delivery. Offer available while quantities last.

Your Privacy: Harlequin Books is committed to protecting your privacy. Our Privacy Policy is available online at www.eHarlequin.com or upon request from the Reader Service. From time to time we make our lists of customers available to reputable third parties who may have a product or service of interest to you. If you would prefer we not share your name and address, please check here. ☐

Help us get it right—We strive for accurate, respectful and relevant communications. To clarify or modify your communication preferences, visit us at www.ReaderService.com/consumerschoice.

HSRLP1

HARLEQUIN®

A Romance

FOR EVERY MOOD™

Spotlight on
Heart & Home

Heartwarming romances
where love can happen
right when you least expect it.

See the next page to enjoy a sneak peek
from Silhouette Special Edition®,
a Heart and Home series.

Introducing McFARLANE'S PERFECT BRIDE
by USA TODAY *bestselling author Christine Rimmer,*
from Silhouette Special Edition®.

Entranced. Captivated. Enchanted.

Connor sat across the table from Tori Jones and couldn't help thinking that those words exactly described what effect the small-town schoolteacher had on him. He might as well stop trying to tell himself he wasn't interested. He was powerfully drawn to her.

Clearly, he should have dated more when he was younger.

There had been a couple of other women since Jennifer had walked out on him. But he had never been entranced. Or captivated. Or enchanted.

Until now.

He wanted her—*her,* Tori Jones, in particular. Not just someone suitably attractive and well-bred, as Jennifer had been. Not just someone sophisticated, sexually exciting and discreet, which pretty much described the two women he'd dated after his marriage crashed and burned.

It came to him that he…he *liked* this woman. And that was new to him. He liked her quick wit, her wisdom and her big heart. He liked the passion in her voice when she talked about things she believed in.

He liked *her.* And suddenly it mattered all out of proportion that she might like him, too.

Was he losing it? He couldn't help but wonder. Was he cracking under the strain—of the soured economy, the McFarlane House setbacks, his divorce, the scary changes in his son? Of the changes he'd decided he needed to make in his life and himself?

Strangely, right then, on his first date with Tori Jones, he didn't care if he just might be going over the edge. He was having a great time—having *fun*, of all things—and he didn't want it to end.

Is Connor finally able to admit his feelings to Tori,
and are they reciprocated?
Find out in MCFARLANE'S PERFECT BRIDE
by USA TODAY bestselling author Christine Rimmer.
Available July 2010,
only from Silhouette Special Edition®.

SSEEXP0710

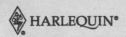
HARLEQUIN®

LESLIE KELLY
Naturally Naughty

Wicked & Willing

On sale June 8

Reader favorites from the most talented voices in romance

Save $1.00 on the purchase of 1 or more Harlequin® Showcase books.